reefs lie here.

Mas y fuera Isle.

Drake's unused channel.

Drake's Isl-
-and.

wrecks

This is tide-swept rocky waste.

West Roarer Rock.

wrecks

ls & banks

ner or naval harbour

The old city.

mountains lie here, far away.

THE
TAKING OF THE GRY

THE
TAKING OF THE GRY

BY

JOHN MASEFIELD

LONDON: WILLIAM HEINEMANN LTD

FIRST PUBLISHED 1934

PRINTED IN GREAT BRITAIN
AT THE WINDMILL PRESS, KINGSWOOD, SURREY

TO
MY WIFE

THE TAKING OF THE GRY

THE events of the Great War have made men forget the Civil War in Santa Ana. But in 1911 war, being rare, was "news" in the newspapers, and even that little civil war made a stir. Some of its events were much talked of at the time; this event of the *Gry* won its hearers.

I can tell you about the *Gry* better than most people. I am going to set it down here before I am too old. I was concerned in her taking. These writing fellows have added things to the tale and made it seem not simple: it was simple.

You all know the Eastern Spanish Main, the Tierra Firme, with its coast and the mountains behind it. People go there for the winter cruises now: and no wonder, for each Republic is wonderful in its own way: Meruel, to the east, rather stern, rich in iron; then, further west, Santa Barbara, rich in copper; then, still further west, Santa Ana, rich in all things. Beyond these, to the west, are what we call the old Republics, those which first broke with Spain. There is no country more marvellous than Spain, nor any that has left such a mark.

She has left three things behind her wherever she has gone, a story, a faith and a dignity.

I am a sailor by profession. As soon as I had a certificate I moved to get into the sun on the Tierra Firme. I was given a berth in one of Green & Silvers' ships (Da Silva, it had been, but the last Da Silva married young Green). You will have heard of Green & Silver, of the Spanish Main Trade, perhaps. They were pioneers from over a hundred years ago, having begun in the sugar trade. They carried the mails and did a regular service right along that coast, from Vera Cruz to Trinidad, one slow ship, stopping at each port, every week, and one fast ship, touching at only the big ports, once a fortnight. We were the only line on the coast at that time: and no doubt the firm made money: we had all the passengers, all the mails and all the carrying trade. I was not much interested in that side of it. I was interested in the Tierra Firme, and in getting to be a pilot to the coast. There was no pilot service there, then, except in Santa Barbara, the men in our service had to pilot the ships themselves.

I started Fourth in the *Malinche,* the oldest and slowest ship in the fleet; but what joy to

2

have the chance. There was fever here and there, of course, and sometimes the rains were a nuisance; still, this is life, where it doesn't do to expect too much. In exchange for it all, there was the piloting. Some lucky men have the job of being pilot up and down a thousand miles of river. Perhaps they are bored by having it all the time. I had it only once in every other day or so like a pearl after a long stretch of string: but it was joy when it came.

You may imagine what it feels like to be on the bridge drawing near to your port, all keyed up to bring her in in style, watching for the marks on the coast, and listening for the surf on the outlier.

I loved it best before dawn, when coming in to a land as dark as indigo, with the faintest of colour pale in the sky above. There would be the forward well and the fo'c's'le lit by the masthead light, the back of the look-out man craned over the dodger, and the gleam of the water spreading from the bows. I loved that picture of the bows and all the tenseness of those near me, the leadsmen, so trusted and sure, in the dickeys at the bridge-ends, ready for quick casts, and the quartermaster's face above the wheel, in the glow of the binnacle

3

lights, with his eyes steady on his mark or on his card. Perhaps the Old Man or the Second Officer would be on the bridge with me: sometimes there would be passengers just below the bridge, shuffling about in the chill and dew, to see the ship go in. Some men fond of power love speaking to an audience, and holding it by what is living in themselves: others love the rule of an orchestra and choir, and the bringing out of music from them. To myself, the joy is the handling of a big ship in a difficult passage, all beset with reefs, and the knowledge that my clear head will carry her clear and set her down at her marks.

I got into the way of making in my mind an image of each channel and harbour as it looked under water and as it looked above. I got to know each place as (shall we say) the seal or the gannet or the osprey might know it. To this day, if I close my eyes, I can reel out in a panorama, in its own colour, with most of its detail, a thousand miles of the Tierra Firme, from Las Palomas to Monte, cape after cape, bay after bay, light and mark and breaking reef, and still see the under-water rocks in each anchorage, and know how much space I have between the keel and them. When

4

I get to the other world, I hope that there will be some difficult channels, not properly charted, so that when I take the angels cruising I may be of use.

Of all the republics along that thousand miles, I liked best that of Santa Ana, which borders Santa Barbara to the west. It is one of the new republics. It is small, as the New World goes; it has a coast of four hundred miles, and no great depth. But it has a driving, stirring climate, without a rainy season, and the people are as stirring and delightful as the climate. A great many English have gone there during the past hundred and fifty years: some of them took part in the war of independence: Almirante Browne is on their postage stamps to this day.

Long before I went to those parts, I knew about Almirante Browne. His people came from the Shropshire side of the Welsh border, near Caer Ocvran. His sister married my great-great-grandfather. We had a miniature of the Almirante at Assendon St. Mary. As a little boy, collecting postage stamps, I used to compare it with the stamps, which of course showed a much older man. People used to talk vaguely in my presence about "our Santa Ana relations," for there were descendants of the Almirante. I never expected to see any of them: but, in time, I did.

As Santa Ana is a rugged land, with bad inland communications, they use the sea a great deal; more than any nation, and have many little ports and two big ones; Santa Ana, the capital and El Puño the naval port. I shall mention both later.

Under Spain, this State was a part of the Province of Santa Barbara, but it split away from Santa Barbara when it broke from Spain, and has ever since been fiercely independent. Santa Barbara has often schemed to bring her back within the fold. It may be that old Don Manuel, the Dictator, with his wisdom and force, might have contrived this, but he died, and his successors, the tame elected presidents, have made it impossible. Their blunderings and threatenings so scared the Santanoes, that they built themselves a Navy.

This Santa Ana Navy is English in tone, (being English-trained) and very good.

The two countries make very touchy neighbours. Green & Silvers wanted Santa Barbara to swallow up the other; many English people did. My own wishes were all the other way.

6

When once I had seen the Santanoes, I was all for them and their independence: they are brisk, stirring fellows, twice the men these Barbarians are.

All through my childhood, as it happened, I had thought of those two lands, because in my father's library I found a copy of Nathaniell Clutterbucke's *Golden Voiage of Sir Francis Drake* to both the ports: it was one of my favourite books. In especial, I loved to read how Drake, being barred out of Santa Barbara Harbour, by a boom across the Mouth, yet sought out and found another entrance by sounding cautiously through the outer reefs. By this channel he towed his fleet into the haven and took the city. "That maze or Troya of rockes and shelfes (did) show forth to his sounders a waie or channel."

When I entered Green & Silvers' employ, I too entered those ports. I shall not forget how I looked out for the reefs through which Drake passed. I saw them first in a romping easterly gale that showed them at their finest, with every rock breaking water. You may be sure that as soon as I had leisure, with weather permitting, I went out to that "maze or Troya" to examine it for myself, with the aid of an old chart, made by a Lieut. D. G. Sevenine, R.N., of H.M. Survey Brig *Boxer*, 1811.

Sevenine must have been deeply interested in Drake. He took the trouble to trace out the only possible course by which Drake could have brought his fleet through the rocks; he marks it "Drake's Channel," with the shrewd marginal comment that it must be a part of a submerged river-mouth, the channel being the bed of the river and the reefs the banks.

About twelve years before I went there, the old Dictator planned to make Drake's Channel a fairway or entrance to the naval harbour; he began work upon it, but his successors shrank from the expense, and abandoned it, with the remark: "Why bother?"

I shall have more to say later about this Channel. At this point, I will say only that it was thrilling to me to be near it, and to be at sea upon that coast, taking ships into and out of harbour. To be in the sun and the freedom, away from dirt, fog and poverty, trying the strength of one's youth, what more could man ask?

On my second passage east, I asked the Old Man if he would let me take her in to Santa Ana. As I showed him that I knew the marks, he let me, and I did it. He was not one to show approval warmly. He growled, with his usual anger at the conditions of the service, "Ah, if you can find your way about like this, they'll let you be a cab-driver in London, when they sack you from the sea." He said no word of praise then, but, later, when we were on the bridge together, he said, "Do you know the Puño marks?"

"Yes, sir," I said, "the merchant-service harbour."

"Ah," he said. "And Santa Barbara?"

"Yes, sir; all the outer anchorage."

"You've got a good memory."

"For the marks on a chart, sir, and for the lights on a coast."

"Yes," he growled, "and how if the lights aren't there, in a fog?"

"I would try a grope with a lead, sir."

"Yes," he said, bitterly. "That's what we all try sooner or later, and pile her up on a reef or put her down the well, and get the sack from the sea for it. We'll be in Santa Barbara after midnight on this trip. We'll see if you can take her in there."

"Thank you, sir, I'm sure I can, sir."

"Youth's a sight too sure, if you ask me,"

9

he growled. "And after forty years of it, you'll find nothing sure except a workhouse ward. Do you know Meruel Passage?"

"Yes, sir, marks and soundings and bearings."

"Wait till you have to take it on a thick night; when the company will sack you if you funk it and the Board of Trade will sack you if you muss it. What did you come to sea for?"

"Fun, sir," I said, "and I didn't get on with my father."

"Well," he growled, "a man who goes to sea for fun would go to hell for pastime. Where did you learn these things? In the *Tierra Firme Pilot?*"

"Partly, sir. I've got the *Pilot:* and then the charts are pretty good: and then I've been into all the ports twice now."

"And you speak Spanish pretty well, I notice."

"I understand it better than I speak it, sir."

"Well: you can't get along without it here, that's sure," he said. "It's said to be a pretty tongue; but the way they sing it is a dog-whine, when it isn't a caterwaul. They got that from the Arabs, they say. They're a good lot on

10

the coast, but they're foreigners when all is said."

"Yes, sir."

"If you'll take a fool's advice," he said suddenly, "you'll get ashore before the sea's got you. Get your hooks into something solid like a copper-mine. There are chances here on the coast, to a young man like you, so that you needn't spend your days sweating another man's ship from port to port. Think of it, Mister, before it's too late. The sea's like rheumatism or marriage: it gets you before you know it: and it's hard to drop."

"Yes, sir," I said, quietly.

"Are you thinking of trying for a job ashore?" he asked.

"I hadn't thought of it, sir."

"Well, thought's the last thing you ask a Fourth Officer for, according to the Catechism," he said. He nodded to me, and went below growling. He was a testy old bear, about to be retired at the age of sixty-five, and angry about it.

We went on to Santa Barbara. We were delayed by a roaring norther off the Cape, so didn't reach the Outer Reefs till after two in the morning of a black wild day with a real

11

surf on the outliers. It was clear enough, but with such a sea running you get odd casts of a lead. I took her in to her marks there. They called the Old Man when we got the bearings for entrance. They told me that on being called he sat up, asked, "Is Mr. Tarlton on the bridge?" and on being told "Yes," just growled, "Well, why call me? He can take her in, better than I can," and then turned over and went to sleep again.

We had a busy forenoon there. The Captain went ashore soon after breakfast, while we were busy at all our hatches getting cargo in or out, checking, tallying and keeping an eye on the gangs. I did not know it and had no suspicion of it, but while he was ashore the Old Man talked to young Mr. Green about me. He knew, though I did not, that the fourth in the *Oquendo,* one of our crack ships, was swallowing the anchor for a shore job: he strongly recommended me for the billet; for though I was junior in the service I could pilot and talk the language. Young Mr. Green came aboard with the Old Man just before lunch, while I was tallying cocoa bags on the fore-hatch. As it happened, just as he reached the bridge above me I spotted the native tallier delivering a short sling, and rounded on him in my best Spanish. It was just the sheerest luck that I had seen the dodge and that young Green should have been there at that instant, but it confirmed him in the opinion that the Old Man had fostered in him. At knock-off time, Mr. Green sent for me into the Old Man's cabin.

Young Mr. Green was a lad of much charm, still modest from youth and a little shy from inexperience. He said how much pleased the Firm always was when an officer showed a special aptitude, and how glad they were to have talent in their officers, and how they liked to show their gladness, etc.; I am an older bird now, but first praise is as sweet as first love pretty nearly. In the end, he said that he hoped that I would continue with the Firm, and would I care to go fourth in the *Oquendo*, there in the bay, waiting for the evening mails before going West? I said I would be glad to go in the *Oquendo*, and thanked him for his kindness. "Well, Mr. Tarlton," he said, "I am glad, and I hope you will be happy in her. We have lost a great many officers lately, who have found posts ashore; and we want to show our junior

13

officers that if they will stay with us we will watch over them and see that they are not losers by it." After that, he shook hands and went ashore. "You'll shift into the *Oquendo* straight away, Mr. Tarlton," he said, as he went down the ladder, "as soon as you can get your gear together."

When he had gone, my Old Man took a turn with me. "You have your chance now," he said. "If you care to take it. The boss has his eye on you: and you're shoved into the flagship before you've been on the coast a year. You don't want to believe all the guff a Company coughs about 'watch over' and 'not be a loser.' A Company's a thing with neither a stern to be kicked nor a soul to be saved, if you ask me. If they would pay their officers a living wage and give them a decent life, they wouldn't find them leaving the service. However, you're a young fellow, Tarlton, in your first success. It's not much good saying this to you, is it?"

"No, sir," I said. "But I do thank you for your kindness in recommending me to Mr. Green for promotion."

"An ass I was, if you ask me," he growled. "I lose a fine young officer, and now shall have some other griff just finished pinching raisins. I'll have to watch him and train him and do his job for him. My steward's packed your things for you while I've been talking; and your gear's in the boat, and the boat's waiting. When an owner expects you to shift in five minutes, shift in two, and he'll say a nice thing to you and as like as not reduce your salary." We shook hands: I went down the ladder and pulled away from the *Malinche*, to the *Oquendo*, a 7,000-ton ship, our Commodore's flag, where I reported to the Commodore, old Roarer Bosbury, a great big lion of a man. "Ha," he roared at me, "so you're the lad who can pilot blindfold. Come on into my room a moment, till you sign. The steward'll shift your gear. And now that you've signed," he added, a minute later, "I want you to nip into the boat with this letter for old Mr. Weycock. Give it into his hands and wait for his answer, then come straight back aboard, will ye?"

"Yes, sir," I said, so down I went to the *Oquendo's* boat and away. I had been hard at it in a hot sun for five hours and had had no "dinner," but duty is duty. As I went, I saw what a change the *Oquendo* was going to

15

be for me: a man of war gig to go ashore in, with a reservists crew; a quartermaster to salute at the gangway head, the men leaping to an order everywhere, (all of them reservists) and the ship like a new pin. I liked the little that I had seen of the Roarer. Some big sailors are all outside, the hearty dog, the breezy admiral type. The Roarer was at first sight much such an one, with a big red face, a broad smile, great white teeth, a shock of white hair, and the rest of it. Later, I saw how excellent a sailor he was and how wise a man.

As I came back to the gig, with my answer from Mr. Weycock, I noticed on the Mole a man a little older than myself, waiting at the stairhead, with a couple of tin uniform cases beside him. He turned towards me, as I drew near, and at once I set him down as a naval officer, and one whom I had somewhere seen before: I could not imagine where. He was about five feet eight or nine in height, with a sailor's face, and a look such as I have only seen on the faces of sailors who have a reckless resolution and courage. It is a humorous, dare-devil cock of the eye more than anything; or some odd combination of the look of the mouth and eye together. It can no more be

16

described than genius can be. When it is once seen it is recognised, and any officer having it can carry a crew into hell and back again and round the North Pole for pastime.

He came up to me at once with a frank and charming air, that would have won a mutineer, and said in excellent English: "I have missed the tender, and am going in the *Oquendo* to Puño. If you are going off to her, will you take me off?"

I said that I would be delighted and would he step into the gig, as I was going off at once. So my cox put his cases into the gig and invited him down.

He hopped into the boat with a sailor's grace and certainty. "It is like old times," he said, "to be in an English gig, with a brass yoke and white lines. I was trained by your men, you see."

"Are you in the Navy here, then?" I asked.

"No. Santa Ana," he said. "But let me introduce myself. I'm Browne. They always called me 'Tom Brown' in your Navy, from a book. I have other names. They pronounce it Bronnay here."

"I suppose you're descended from the Almirante," I said. And as I spoke, I knew

17

that he was, because that old miniature at home was the very image of him.

"The chap on the postage stamps, the Liberator? Yes. He was my great-great-grandfather. You see, I have English ancestry."

"I know," I said. "And as it happens, Mr. Browne, we're related in a sort of way, very distantly. Your ancestor's sister married a Tarlton."

"Of Assendon St. Mary, in Berkshire," he said.

"Yes," I said, "more Ass than Saint, they say in Berkshire. My name is Tarlton, and that's where I come from. We've got a miniature of your great-great-grandfather. He was my great-great-grand-uncle."

"I went to Assendon St. Mary once," he said, in a queer voice. I knew, from the way in which he spoke, that my father, who is an odd fish, to say the least of it, had been rude to him for being a Catholic, or for some other crazy reason, or for no reason at all. I knew that there must have been some trouble, for I had never heard of the visit of a Santa Ana cousin: if the visit had been a success I should have been told of it.

"My father is a collector," I said, meaning

18

that this might explain his inhumanity.

"He doesn't seem to collect foreign relatives," he answered. We looked at each other and grinned. "I do," I said, "that is, if I may." He grinned: and asked, in Spanish, if I spoke that tongue and how long I had been upon the coast. After that, we talked in Spanish till we drew near to the *Oquendo*.

Though I did not know it, the Roarer was watching for me to see how I brought the gig alongside. The boat had been reported to him and he was there, looking out. Well, I can do most things with a boat: and being anxious to impress this new sort of cousin, who had been in the English Navy, and seeing that I had a rare good crew, I told them to give way for a flying moor.

The *Oquendo* was lying head to sea at the Green & Silver moorings. I brought the boat round on her port side and across her bows, giving way like blazes. As we came round to starboard, I judged my time, said "In bow," shifted my helm, told my starboard oars to hold water and my port oars to give way; and the gig swerved round almost in her own length and sidled into the gangway just as I said "Toss your oars."

19

"Jolly neatly done, Charlie," my new cousin whispered: "And if your starboard oar had caught a crab you'd have ripped her straik off."

"My starboard oar can't catch a crab," I muttered under my breath. Then I followed him up the gangway.

The Roarer was waiting for me at the gangway head. He knew Browne, for he said, "Ha, my Teniente, I'm glad to see you. Steward, see that Lieutenant Browne is at my table to-night." Then turning to me, he said: "You have the answer?" After he had read it, he said, "Since when have you been doing Admiral's Swerves, may I ask?"

"Only since I've had a first-rate crew, sir," I answered. He was pleased with the answer, I thought.

"I haven't seen it done since Admiral Hornby's time," he said. "And that's forty-odd years ago. It's a very pretty thing if it's done judgmatically. And you had a critic in the boat with you. Teniente Bronnay is some sailorman. By the way, you haven't had any lunch, have you?"

"No, sir," I said, "but that doesn't matter."

"Ah, but it does matter," he said. "Steward,

20

show Mr. Tarlton to the mess and see that he has everything he needs."

He did not comment on my flying moor, but I could see that he was pleased with me. I had had some little experience of captains and mates by that time and knew how apt they are to judge by a first impression. I had made a good first impression, and vowed to maintain it.

I shall never forget that first day in the *Oquendo,* so different from anything that I had known, so smart, and so much style in the way of carrying-on, and everything going smoothly and swiftly, entirely from the Captain's will. In doing his will was the peace of everyone: trouble fell instantly on the man who didn't.

It was, I think, in the second dog-watch, that same evening, that my cousin caught me for a walk. The Roarer had sent for me a little while before, when we got under way, to see what I knew of the pilotage; and I was given the job of taking her out. It was easy enough in clear daylight, to one who knew the marks. I did not need a cast of the lead, though I took one or two. The Roarer did not praise my performance, but gave the negative praise of saying that some men never seemed to get the hang of it. We passed close to the *Malinche*, which already looked very small and mean and old-fashioned to me. I had had happy times in her. I thought, "What fun, when I get the command of a ship like the *Malinche* and take her in and out and up and down on this most beautiful coast till I die or retire." It did not seem possible to me then, that one could ever tire of the beauty and the change, the sea breaking, the engines beating and the men ready; with the ship like a horse in control ready for whatever was asked of her.

Bronnay met me on deck in my watch below: we walked together. In my own speech I should say that we "mooched" together, that is, we walked slowly and found ourselves pouring out our hearts to each other. We were drawn together from the first as young men will be: we liked the cuts of each other's jibs; we were both sailors (and there is only one sea-service in spite of the guns and gold-lace) and then the far distant dim relationship gave us the feeling that many of the barriers, of race and faith and custom, were down from between us.

22

He told me that his mother and he were the only Brownes now alive, that he had been naval attaché at Washington for a year, then for the last few days, on his return from Washington, he had been on a special mission in Santa Barbara, and that he expected war before long.

This was in 1911, when most Englishmen and I think Americans, too, believed that war was a thing of the past among the civilised nations. (We had had one apiece quite recently.) So I said: "War? Rubbish. Who on earth would pick a quarrel with you, and why?"

"Santa Barbara would, to-morrow," he answered. "We're the plum and she's the greed. She wants to annex us. And have you seen our President?"

"President de Leyva? Yes, I saw him drive by once in Santa Ana."

"What did you think of him?" Tom asked, as though my opinion were really worth having.

"I only saw him drive by," I said. "I thought he was a fine-looking man: rather stiff and proud, I should say. He had an escort in his own livery, blue and silver, which seemed odd in a Republic."

"Stiff and proud, yes;" he said, "and bent on handing over our Republic to Santa Barbara. He has just been re-elected, as you know, for a second term, by a majority of seven votes. What power and support he lacks in Santa Ana he will buy in from Santa Barbara. He is rich and has enormous bribes from these foreign concessionaires. So he and Santa Barbara will declare for Annexation, and we of the Santa Ana Navy will fight them on it."

"Really?" I said, "and when?"

"Pretty soon," he said. "No, Charlie," he added, "for I shall call you Charlie, if you'll call me Tom, I think it will be very soon. He'll try to purge the Navy of those most opposed to him, and we shall fight."

"That's a pretty serious matter, rebellion," I said.

"Being in earnest is serious," he said. "But we don't call it rebellion. You in Europe have political parties centred in the Army. We here have a party centred in the Navy. And if he and his gang of foreign concessionaires try to force us to submit, we'll fight."

"I don't quite see how you can say that it isn't rebellion," I said. "You as a Navy are

24

a Service of the State, pledged by oath to serve the State."

"We are servants of the Constitution, sworn to uphold the Constitution," he replied. "And any violation of the Constitution shall be fought."

"The world will call it Mutiny," I said. "And I don't see how the Navy will fight the State and the Army."

"Be patient," he said with a grin. "You will see, before very long. We're quite a good lot in the Santa Ana fleet."

"Yes, I've noticed that," I answered. "But if you have the Santa Barbara fleet against you, as well as the Santa Barbara army, and the Santa Ana army, and the whole of both states as well, it will be rocky going, won't it? What is the Santa Barbara fleet like? We suppose it to be pretty good."

"It was pretty good, under the old Dictator," he said. "We don't think it good now. But even if it were good, it should not dictate to us."

"I suppose you'll be in the thick of it," I said.

"If I don't get rounded up beforehand as a suspect," he answered. "Wouldn't you leave this, and join us, Charlie, and come and serve with me?"

"It wouldn't do," I said. "A foreigner would be always suspect in a Navy or in any service during a war. But if I can help at any time, I will, you know that."

I did not think when I spoke those words that I should so soon be called upon to help.

We did not talk more at that time because the Roarer came up to claim him and I sheered off, out of respect. But I watched him walking up and down, and though I had known him for but a few hours I would have died for him even then. He had that charm of manner, and that cock of the eye and head, no man that I ever saw could resist him. I was very young, then, and had not at that time known the joy of a close companion, which is the great joy that youth offers. My heart was full of him, I tell you.

I had for months heard that the two Republics were suspicious of each other. I hadn't heeded the talk: now suddenly it became all important to me and to everybody. All were talking of it. I became aware that our passengers were already arrayed in sides, ready to kill each other. I saw some Santa Ana men watching Tom as he walked. It was plain that they were of the President's party, wishing him dead. I saw some Barbarians watching those same men, plainly wishing them dead.

Late that night there was a row in the steerage, where a Barbarian insulted a Santanoe, who drew some sharp-edged tool, probably a razor, and slashed him with it. One of the stewards stopped the fray by knocking their heads together. The Roarer thought it wiser to double the stewards' watch in the steerage that night, though that particular quarrel went no further. The Barbarian was put into the sick bay: he deserved all the trouble that came to him, we thought. He had played the trick (common among the Germans before the war) of trying to stare the Santanoe out of countenance. However, those who play with fire get burned in the end, though sometimes others get burned first.

Tom was well-known to the officers in our mess: "Bronnay is back," they were saying. "He's been in these Embassies. Now that he's back, they'll be having their civil war, you'll find."

I saw that he was liked and admired: all our officers were after him for a talk or a walk whenever they were off duty, and I must say that I was jealous of them. I, as junior officer, got the smallest allowance of him, but at odd instants I came across him and each instant thrilled me.

He had a way of blarneying the Roarer that no other man could approach. He even won him into allowing him to come on to the bridge the next morning to see me take the ship into Catoche, which is an evil place, on the point of that name, a real Ship's Graveyard where we used to land mails if the surf were not too bad. It is all sown with jags that break or don't break. On that morning, they were breaking: and a man casting a glance at all that angry water would swear that no channel exists: however, it is simple enough, if you have a clear head.

It was my job to do it: someone had told the Roarer that I could do it: he was there on the bridge beside me: and I suddenly realised that he knew that I could do it, and would not interfere; and at once my heart leapt up, for the Roarer was a very fine seaman and his trust in an officer not lightly given. "All right, my Captain," I said to myself, "you trust me, and I'll not let you down." The Roarer took

Tom to the side of the bridge and left me in control: they laughed and chatted while I brought her in, and held her while we landed and received our mails, and then brought her out, to continue the run to Puño.

Tom congratulated me afterwards. "I'd heard that you are a pilot," he said. "You certainly are."

"When you get to Puño," I asked him, "will you be sent afloat, do you think?"

"I shan't land at Puño," he answered. "I've had my orders here. I'm coming on with you to Santa Ana, to join the flagship, the *Almirante O'Duffy*. All the fleet is there at present."

"Well," I said, "I'm glad I'm to see some more of you than I had expected."

"About that matter that we were discussing last night," he said, "I don't think the explosion I mentioned will be very long delayed. In other words, the glass is falling."

"I'm sorry to hear that," I said.

"Well, perhaps the sooner the better," he answered. "Like your own Admiral I wish the war would end, so that we could get the men back to battle-practice."

29

Puño is the naval station for a good many reasons. There is coal in some of the valleys near it and excellent iron in others. There is a very good natural harbour, which they have improved. They have abundant building and repairing slips, and a fine dry dock, the only one on the Santa Ana coast.

It is not an attractive place: I don't know any naval port that is. The hills near it are somewhat bare and reddish. The naval barracks, parade grounds and gun-testing ranges are like most such things, neat and hideous.

Well, we landed and received mails and passengers, in the usual racket of winches and launches; then we went on again towards Santa Ana. By this time, I was settled down (or screwed up to) the life in the *Oquendo*. I had time for talks with Tom; many jolly talks.

"I told you that the explosion would be soon," he said. "It will be this month, I think. The President will open the Cortes, that will be the first step. Then he will say that rumours reach him, which he cannot believe, that the Navy is disaffected, and that though this is probably the invention of evilly disposed persons he would be failing in his high duty, etc., to the Republic if he did not make enquiry.

That will be the second step. Then he will state (probably the next day) that he learns with deep regret, that some at least of the suspicions are too well-founded, and that he feels bound to appoint a Committee of Public Safety. After that, anything may happen."

"What do you, yourself, think will happen?" I asked.

"Probably, they will order that all officers of the Army and Navy shall take an oath of loyalty and obedience. The Army will take it first, with enthusiasm, then it will be our turn. It will be an oath that we can never accept; so that that will bring matters to a head."

"And the fleet will be in Santa Ana at the time?"

"Probably."

"Under the guns of the forts?"

"Yes, and under the howitzers of the President's brother officers in the gunners. We're not afraid of those things. If the Navy will hold together, and it will, we shall do them, I hope."

Afterwards, I had a talk with the Roarer. "So you've found a cousin on board?" he said. "A fine young fellow, your cousin. I could wish for both your sakes that he wasn't in their

31

Navy, for there's trouble ahead, from what I can see. There are a lot of big firms pressing Santa Barbara to annex. That old rogue elephant in the Copper Combine is at the bottom of that. I don't like the looks of it. Then their President, de Leyva, is bent on the annexation. He'll drive the Navy into mutiny. Then Santa Barbara will step in and start to annex."

"Do you think she'll succeed, sir?" I asked.

"It's hard to say what will happen when a war begins," he answered. "It will end our sailings for a while. Then there'll be floating mines all over the place for a year or more, whatever happens. Still, it hasn't started yet."

The Roarer made up his mind from conversations up and down the coast: he never read a newspaper. He had always a shrewd perception of what the nations were aiming at. The other officers (and the engineers) of the *Oquendo* did not believe that there could be trouble. "These foreigners are just like children," they said. "Civil War? They'll never go to Civil War. They are all too happy and busy making money to think of any such thing. Besides, the foreign business firms would never allow it."

I was junior officer, or I would have said that many foreign business firms might even foster such a thing, as exceedingly good for their particular business.

Well, in the glorious bright morning we came into Santa Ana, right under the old Spanish fort which had fired at Drake and Vernon and so many other English seamen. As we drew in, the usual swarm of boats and launches darted down upon us; and almost before we were on our marks the steam picket-boat of the *Almirante O'Duffy* was alongside for Tom. He gravely saluted me as the boat took him past our bows, and I must say, my heart was torn at losing him.

However, duty called: mail to shift; a hundred and fifty tons of baggage to ship; all the winches going at every hatch and the junior there to be jumped on if anything went wrong anywhere. In the early afternoon, we were away again: and as I took her out, my leadsman reported that the *Almirante O'Duffy* was signalising.

The Teniente Bronnay, it seemed, was wishing the *Oquendo* a pleasant voyage.

We went away west, to all the ports of the story books, and then turned for the east again, visiting port after port, like so many jewels on a string, and changing passengers and mails at each. Presently we were back again in Santa Ana in time for the opening of the Cortes.

Tom came on board to see me soon after we moored.

"It will be very soon, now," he said. "If you go ashore this afternoon you'll see the Cortes opened, which will be the first Act. You'll remember, won't you, that the President's party are called Progresos (short for Progresivos) and our party, the Navy, are the Puros? They're reds: we're blues: don't forget."

I promised that I wouldn't.

I went ashore that afternoon to see the opening of the Cortes; and got a place at the foot of the steps leading to the Parliament House, which was a mean place then, like a morgue, or a tomb to some tenth-rate stockbroker in a suburban cemetery.

There was a big crowd, strangely silent for so merry a people.

The steps had been railed off for the women-folk of the members, who stood there wearing party colours, red for the Progresos, blue and white stripes for the Puros. A lot of men wear-

ing red were near the steps. There were many
guardias in the Square, all in their best
uniforms, with swords and white gloves.
Soldiers lined the approaches.

It was a well-ordered business, and
punctual, like all things in Santa Ana.

A few minutes before three the members of
the Cortes arrived, generally two or three together, all looking nervous and self-conscious
when they saw the crowd, and much more so
when they received the crowd's jeers and
cheers.

The leader of the Puros, Admiral Beaumont-
Vincente, came in alone, a fine-looking man, I
thought; calm, quick and dignified: it was said
that his ancestors were some English Vincents.
The women of the Reds hissed him and insulted
him as he went up the steps: I thought that
some of them even tried to spit at him, but
from want of practice or skill didn't make
much of a success of it. Then as people were
cheering and surging and laughing, there came
shouts, the click of bayonets, the clatter of
hoofs, and the order "Off hats." Instantly, the
bands of the Red Regiments, all stationed on
the roofs of the Government buildings, struck
up the National Anthem of Santa Ana:

"I will sing of thy glory, Santa Ana,"

and played through the first stanza. Then, changing, they played softly, the first stanza of the National Anthem of Santa Barbara:

"We will rally round the banner of our fathers,"

which has something of the same rhythm. Then, having delighted all there who were eager for the amalgamation, they played a third tune, unmistakably a mixture of the two airs. At this the claqueurs roared their cheers, Long Live Santa Barbara, Long Live the Sister Saints, Long Live the Brother Presidents. At this point ladies loosed out of the windows the banners of the two lands, linked with crowns. The claqueurs cheered, the bands played louder, with drums and brass. Then in the tumult of the excitement, there came suddenly the salute, a quick thrilling trot of the cavalry of the guard, and the President's carriage drove up. Red carpets unrolled as by magic, red petals fell in showers, red confetti came down like rain, the President went up the steps into the Cortes, and so the Cortes for that day assembled.

After all this I went to the water front, wondering if I could get a boat to the *Almirante O'Duffy* for a word with Tom. On the water front there were a good many Puros, wearing blue and white rosettes, looking at the distant ships in the naval anchorage. I was stopped by a guardia at the steps: he wished to know what I wanted and on being told, said, that no man not in naval uniform was allowed to visit any ship in the fleet. So at this I walked to the Naval Club and asked if Tom were there. The Club was almost deserted: and the porter said that the Teniente Browne was on service.

Coming down to the water front, I saw that the *Oquendo* was flying her Recall signal, so I took a boat with two rowers and pulled off to her at once: and a nice hurrah's nest I found there, with people flooding on board as though the town were on fire.

I asked old Peters: "What on earth is the rally?"

"Rally," he said; "they've got a sudden scare that the Navy is going to shell the town. This began at two o'clock, and every berth on board is full and over-full. We're rigging a guardsman's bedroom in each well and Red Sea Pilgrim's lavatories over the sides. Get to it."

I did get to it, thinking that Tom had foretold a Naval scare as a part of the First Act. However, I had no time to think about it then. In addition to the booked passengers we had seven hundred people on board in every stage of panic and confusion. We rushed things through quicker than I have ever seen them done since, triced up our ladders to keep some hundreds of others from crowding on board, and so got away into a gathering gale, which helped us to sort the poor creatures, as a gale will. I had too much to do that evening and night, even to worry about Tom. In my bunk presently I thought of him as perhaps already in a war, or being lined-up against a wall to be shot by a squad of Reds.

What worried me was the fact that many of the fat cigar type of passenger, who were travelling not from panic, but from a wish to be out of the way during the troubles, wore red favours openly and seemed to regard the whole thing as going according to plan.

The next morning we put into the road-stead of a little place called Chola Vieja, where the Indians had a city on one of the hills (a queer place: I climbed to it once: a collection of mud huts with old tiles on them) and the Santanoes a copper smeltry and some very fine vineyards. Here, to our great joy, we landed most of our refugees. There is a railway to Chola Vieja from Santa Ana, so that we got the Santa Ana morning paper *La Constitución*, which gave some account of the Cortes, and a leader headed "The President's Just Alarm." I read this with amazement at Tom's foresight. The President had told the Cortes "that he was uneasy at the tone said to be prevalent in the Navy, and that though he could not credit all that had been told him, he felt that he must ask law-abiding citizens to help him to restore public confidence by whatever measures might be necessary. That, in the midst of this in some ways disquieting situation it was comforting to find that the Santa Ana army remained true to its high traditions and might be trusted to the death. That, he assured all citizens of the Republic none but the guilty had anything to fear, that all would yet be well, and that despite the faction of the factions, their Mother State, under the Symbol of the Church and the colours of the battalions, would fulfil her lofty national destiny."

"That's the way to win a sailor's love," the Roarer commented. "To tell him that a soldier's a better fellow."

We went on from Chola Vieja, and past the gorges of great, wild beauty, with cataracts coming over the cliffs, and the crags all green with liana, and patched with white trumpet flowers; most beautiful, but a bad stretch for recurrent fevers, till we came to the settled parts round Cholula. Here they had a telegraph station and a newspaper, *El Libertad*, with the news of a day later. The news said that the President had found that he had no alternative but to demand that all Naval Officers should reattest upon a new form. This was headed "A Righteous Decision." We had a long stay at Cholula, for a great deal of silver was being shipped; we discussed the news in our mess. Peters, our Chief, who was an elderly, very strict, very smart officer, always stretched to four pins in his dress, held that the President, being the head of the State, had a right to demand what oaths he chose from the servants of the State; and that if there were disaffection in a public service like a Navy, the loyalty of its officers should be tested by new oaths, and those who refused the oaths should be broken.

"That is what we should expect in England," he said. "If our Navy should become disaffected, we should proceed in much the same way, surely? The Admiralty would send for the disaffected officers to come ashore, and there they would either have to take the oath or be cashiered. It stands to reason: they could do nothing else."

"It looks a lot more serious than it did," our Second said. "The cables are censored and delayed: and the wireless is jammed, with nothing coming through at all. Well, it won't be a long dispute. The President must be master in his own house. You can't have a public service becoming a State within the State."

The mess, being disciplined men, supported the side of discipline.

No more news came through that evening; and at midnight, having completed with silver and taken on board a foredeck load of fruits and vegetables for Puño, we went out from Cholula towards our next little port of Torre del Duque, where we were due at dawn, to land mails and proceed. We never stayed more than twenty minutes at Torre; a pretty old Spanish city with white fortifications still studded here and there with English cannon-balls.

It was in the early morning of that day, after daybreak, when we had left Torre astern, as I

41   D

was seeing to the washing down, that I had my next thrill. I was just hopping on to our poop, having got the hoses on to the after well, when I caught sight of ships astern. I went quickly to the taffrail, where old Jim, one of the watch, was polishing some brass.

"There's the fleet, sir," he said, nodding towards the ships. "That's the Santa Ana fleet. They've escaped, sir."

I ran forward to the bridge and reported the fleet. The Roarer, who slept "with one eye open and all his soul on the bridge," was on deck as I got my glasses off the hook. He had his glasses on to the ships before I had. "That's the Santa Ana fleet," he said. "Do you know the ships?"

"Not to recognise them, sir."

"You ought to learn the silhouettes of all ships of war," he said, "all the ships of war in the world."

By this time, I had a clear view of those twenty streams of smoke and smudges white at the bows. "Yes, it's the Fleet," the Roarer said. "That's the flag, but she's not the *O'Duffy*, she's the *Almirante Bazan* and her sister ship the *Almirante Moro*. There's the *Colon*: an old cruiser, but new engines in her.

I wonder why the *Almirante O'Duffy* isn't there: she is their crack ship."

"Perhaps they've been fighting, sir, already," I said.

"No," he said, staring through his glasses. "Those ships haven't been fighting. If they'd fought, they'd be all machine-gunned up, like currants in a pudding."

"They're going a good lick, sir," I said.

"Indeed they are," he said.

I did not know anything about naval war at that time (I was soon to learn) and so did not appreciate the fine points of the display that the fleet made. They were preceded by four swift destroyers, all good modern ships heavily armed. Then came six very light unarmoured cruisers in two columns of three, perhaps a mile and a half apart. Then, in line ahead between the columns were the three armoured cruisers which made the main force of the fleet, and seven dispatch-ships and destroyers brought up the rear. All the force was being driven at full speed, at a steady fifteen, and all could do it and keep it, that fact alone made me open my eyes to the power of the Santa Ana Navy. They kept station, too, save that the outer destroyers made swift sheers here and there from time to time. As they hove nearer, I saw that they were admirably painted for service in tropical water: I had not realised before how good their colour was. Their upper works were a pale grey, which continued with increasing paleness to about a yard from the water-line. From that point to below the water-line they are painted with irregular wavings of white. I do not know whether this would be effective in northern waters, but in that light and on those seas it was an admirable protection.

"They're well protected, sir," I said. "Their colour tones into the sea at less than a mile away."

"So I've reported, more than once," the Roarer said. "Well, they're going fin out. They mean business of some sort. They're off to Puño. They're smart seamen, these chaps. They keep station and they're clear for action: all the rails and things down: and the hoses running: see them? Well, I must say, I don't like the look of it. However, I'll give them a dip as they pass."

"Where's my cousin's ship, sir, the *O'Duffy*?" I asked. "I hope she's not been put down."

"I hope not, I'm sure," he said. "But if a

ship gets on to a mine, what else can happen to her?"

There was no answer to that: what else could happen to her? My heart sank down into my boots at the thought of the ship gone and Tom drowned. There was nothing more likely. The President would have taken steps to stop the Flag at all costs.

As I stared at the oncoming ships my eyes filled with tears as the thought of that glorious comrade gone.

Somehow, the word of the fleet's passing had got about among the passengers, all early as it was; a crowd of them gathered at the rails to see them go by. Many of them judged from the fact that the fleet was there, that the President had been defied and that a civil war, or something like it, had begun. I heard the cries of "Los Puros, los perros" (a popular cry then), "Leperos, perros, puros," and other ejaculations of Viva el Presidente. Viva de Leyva. Viva Santa Ana. Viva Las Santas Sorores, etc., etc., according to the political faiths. There came oaths and threats from the more excitable, and sides were swiftly taken and insults exchanged, and then the fleet was past us, driving swiftly on, removing the immediate cause of quarrel. We were not doing at that time more than thirteen; they had the heels of us.

At breakfast later that morning, the talk was all of what had happened, to bring the fleet there. Our wireless man got Trinidad after a time and came in during breakfast to tell us that there was an unconfirmed rumour that the Santa Ana fleet, being dissatisfied with the unconstitutional methods of the President, had renounced their oaths, and had taken the fleet out of Santa Ana harbour, under fire of the forts; and "that a situation of some obscurity existed." Old Peters, the Chief, took the view that they had been guilty of mutiny. I suggested that if the President had exceeded his lawful powers, the fleet had obeyed the law in refusing to obey him. As I was junior there I got it pretty hot, but stuck to it.

"Whatever happens," old Peters said, "we shall be warned off these Santa Ana ports for some time, or till this trouble ends. We shall be warned out of Puño, you'll see; and some of our ships will be laid up, you'll see. It's very bad for business, this kind of tomfoolery, but as it's always done by men who don't work, but are worked for, and as they don't have to foot the bills, it will go on, I suppose. In any case," he added, "I suppose it comes to blows in the end in some quarrels, whatever efforts are made for peace. And in any case this can't go on long: a fleet can't fight the rest of the State."

At this a discussion began; for I, who was all for Tom and Tom's side, maintained that for the matter of that a President and an Army couldn't fight the rest of the State; and that Santa Ana, being a coastline with a mountain range just behind it was at the mercy of a fleet holding the coast.

"Mercy be damned," they said to me. "What can the fleet do? Hold up commerce? I'd like to see them try it. If they try that they'll have all the continental and American powers protesting. What else can they do? Attack Santa Ana? They can't. Ships can't fight forts; that's been proved time and time again. Besides, as likely as not Santa Barbara will come in against them, send a fleet to Puño, mop them up and proceed to make the two lands one."

"I see what will happen," old Peters said. "Nothing spectacular. The fleet will lie at Puño for a while; then the President's agents will bribe the crews into giving up their officers, who will be shot, and then it will all fizzle out."

I suppose that the other men in the mess either believed this, or felt that the Chief should be supported against a junior. They agreed with old Peters that that would be the end of the rebellion. I said that war didn't happen as people expected, but quite otherwise: and that no war yet in history had gone according to plan.

"Well," the Second Officer said, "after all, a large part of war must be supply. If this Navy has rebelled, and you might remember that the rumour isn't yet confirmed, it will only have such supply as the naval base can give, which won't be much. The fleet will be like King Charles I: he may have had right on his side, but he couldn't supply his side and the Parliament could."

"That is so," Peters said. "I give them a week . . . ten days at most . . . Santa Barbara will move, the foreign powers will complain, the chiefs will see their impotence, and they will either escape or be given up. If you ask me, they are just simply pirates."

Well . . . we left the matter there. We

went on in the track of the fleet towards Puño, which we reached towards sunset. As we drew near, a naval despatch ship, a smart steam yacht painted naval grey, with q.f. guns upon her, and flying the S.A. colours, bore down upon us, replied to our salute, and hailed us, that Puño was closed to general traffic, and that we were to avoid an area now mined, that a state of war existed between the Navy and the Presidential forces, and that, in short, we were to follow her straightaway through the dangerous area. There was no mistaking this: war was declared: so we followed as bidden.

The Roarer hailed the officer for news of the *O'Duffy*, but received no answer: no doubt it was a sore point.

We heard no further news till we reached Santa Barbara next day. We were ordered by wireless to avoid Cape Catoche. Our passengers were in a ferment and quarrelled among themselves: I often thought that some of them would come to knives about it, but somehow the Roarer was always there at the critical point and no one had his throat cut. At Santa Barbara, as we came in over the Entrance, our agent boarded us. He had us into the mess and harangued us. "This war which has broken out has not been unforeseen. It has been brewing for a long time and has been prepared for by the Company, who have to expect certain contingencies, which may or may not happen. The chances are that it will not last long without certain interference by other powers. In any case, we of Green & Silvers are and must be neutral: and in order to avoid any difficulty or danger besetting neutrals in time of war our sailings to the Santa Ana ports are cancelled. We must ask you gentlemen to accept the arrangements which have been made for you. As the Santa Ana sailings are cancelled, we shall take this opportunity of putting the *Oquendo* into dry dock at Monte (she being now very grassy), sending the *Hernando Cortes* home, to have her engines repaired, and laying off some of the staff, upon full pay, for the next month, or until the situation clears up a little."

I hung about till the seniors had finished with him, and then asked him if he had had any news of the *Almirante O'Duffy*.

"Yes," he said, "the flagship. She didn't rebel. She was the only ship that didn't."

"Did she stay, then, in Santa Ana?" I asked.

"Yes, of her own will. She's there."

50

"Did they try to take her?" I asked.

"I believe they tried something," he said, "but it was nipped in the bud, I think."

That was all that I could learn from him. It was not cheerful news. I could only suppose that Tom had "tried something" and been "nipped in the bud," probably by a firing squad on the Presidio beach.

However, there was work to be done, to turn the ship over before going down to Monte. I was busy enough all the rest of that day. In the evening, I was told that I was to be laid off, for the present, upon full pay, and that a room was reserved for me at the Club, if I cared to go there: so I went ashore to the Club and took the room, and then in the Club library went through the files of the papers trying to find news of Tom, or of his flagship.

There was no account, that I could find, of any fighting or of people killed or wounded. One paper said that the *Almirante O'Duffy* had been saved to Santa Ana "by the loyalty of her marines and engine-room staff, who had put the disloyal officers ashore and brought the ship under the batteries of the Army."

If this were true, I reckoned that Tom would have been shot. I went out from the

51

reading-room broken-hearted, wandered the streets till I was faint, passed a wretched night at the Club, and in the morning went out again to try to walk off my misery.

I never liked Santa Barbara. It is very grand, very ample and splendid; with squares of palaces and many very beautiful churches; all made under the direction of the old Dictator who died just long enough ago to make his work disgusting to men of to-day. It was a commonplace of talk, that all that he had done was now being undone, and all that he had tautened was now being slackened. But of course, it is beautiful, and the gardens and the aquarium are wonderful, and the old curiosity shops on the sea front, where they sell the old Indian and Spanish things, are worth the going to see; the Indian jars and picture histories, with actual portraits of some of the Conquerors and the iron work of the Conqueror's houses, all these are strange. But in two days I loathed the city and the men in it, and I think life itself. No news of the civil war came through, only the usual leaders by the enemy, that "in a few days the misguided rebels would reap the penalty of their treasons." All opinion in Santa Barbara was dead against the rebels.

The papers urged active intervention, destruction of the rebellious fleet, and "a merging of the two Republics, prelude, let us hope, to the establishment of a United States of the South." I raged at all this. I stood it for two days and then determined to get to sea, so that I should not always be thinking of Tom. I took a boat, and went the round of all the British ships in the port, to ask if they wanted a junior officer. Of course, I had my trouble for nothing. In that time of war and uncertainty the shipping world was over-manned and no one wanted my wares. I saw some fine ships, and met some very rude captains, and pulled back in my shore boat to the Mole. And as I drew near to the stairs, the newsboys suddenly came racing along from the offices, crying that there had been a most bloody naval battle at Santa Ana.

I bought a paper from a boy, found a bench in the shade in the sea-front garden, and read the bare news, received officially from Santa Ana, that the rebellious naval forces had made a determined attack there, to cut out the cruiser, the *Almirante O'Duffy*, which had refused to follow the fleet into rebellion. "The attack," so the account ran, "had been repulsed with heavy loss to the rebels, who had lost their flagship, the *Almirante Moro,* sunk by a Loyalist torpedo." It occurred to me that the rebel flagship was the *Almirante Bazan,* but I knew that the *Moro* was her sister ship, and that her loss would be a cruel blow to Tom's cause. "If this should be true," I thought, "it would mean that their game's about up." I was inclined to think it true, but a kind of glimmer was within me, that the news came from Santa Ana, where many might like it to be thought true. Even before our war I had the wit to doubt "official news." I thought that I would wait till I had seen the next morning's papers and the ticker at the Club. Besides, at the Club one met all sorts of experienced merchants, shippers, consuls as well as seamen, who would in some odd way contrive to get the facts and the inner story before the rest of the world. From them, if I listened adroitly (as I thought) I might gather the truth.

Then I thought, "Couldn't I go to Puño, and join these rebels? Tom's gone, I suppose, but one of his kin might bear a hand for him, and give those devils a knock before the game's up." That old hauling song kept ringing in my ears:

"Tom's gone, so I'll go, too.
Tom's gone to Hilo."

Then I suddenly decided that I would go
to Puño and offer my services. After all I was
qualified, as well as a naval reservist, and quite
willing to serve without pay. I knew that all
sailings to Puño had ceased, but I had money
enough for the railway journey across the
Sierras. At the station they told me that the
bookings had been cancelled, and that the
trans-Sierra trains were no longer running.

The railway men would not or could not
tell me very much. They shrugged their
shoulders, and grimaced and spread their
hands. "Who knows?" "Who can tell?"
"Reasons of State." "No civilian ticket within
fifty miles of the frontier, so it is ordained."
When I asked for a ticket to fifty miles from
the frontier they spread their hands and said:
"There are no trains." When I asked: "When
there would be trains?" they fell back at once
on "Who knows? To-morrow, you ask: perhaps to-morrow."

You will remember the kind of thing from
the days of the War.

I went to the Club, and had a look at the

ticker, which gave no fuller details. The evening papers came in at intervals, all against the Naval rebels, magnifying the President's victory, and urging the Santa Barbara Government to seize this opportunity of bringing the two Republics "into one fraternal fold." Peters came in as I was reading.

"Well," he said, in his dry ramrod manner, looking like one of these soldiers, "your friends have lost the *Moro*. That will about end their rebellion, I take it. The President has the *O'Duffy*, and of course he has all the Army besides."

"The Army won't be much good to him," I said, on the general principle that an army isn't much good to anyone.

"I'm afraid it will shoot your cousin," he said.

"My cousin's dead," I said savagely.

"I'm sorry," he said gently. "But you'd rather that than that he should be shot, as rebels always are."

"Like Oliver Cromwell and George Washington," I called out after him, but I'm afraid the shot missed.

The Club filled up in the evening when the offices closed. Men came in for billiards, or

56

news, or a rubber of bridge. By going from
card-room to billiard-room and then back into
the reading-room, I could get a clear impression of English feeling about the rebellion. It
was all hostile to the receding Navy, almost
without exception. It was all exultant that the
rebels should "have taken a knock." This was
easy to understand, of course. The English
took the national line, that it is unthinkable
that the Navy should rebel. Any Navy that
rebels, they said, ceases to be a Navy, and
becomes a piratical force. "These fellows aren't
rebels now, they're pirates, and it would be
quite in accord with justice that an international force, or the Santa Barbara fleet,
should go in and just mop them up: scupper
the lot of them."

I found this strain of talk very hard to bear.
However, I listened because the talk was often
picturesque and forceful, and helped me to
understand the forces at work and the currents
of policy.

As the night came on, I found the bar the
best place for talk. It was a great cool room,
set about with wicker chairs. The bar was on
one side of it, very bright and clean, with
palms at each end, and negro servants mixing

the cocktails. There were many men there at midnight, and most of the talk was of the rebellion. Presently a big man of early middle age came in. He was in full evening dress, and even in that showed a costliness and a rarity not usual on the coast. He was very handsome, and yet there was a wild look about his eyes which showed that he was a drinker. He was somewhat flushed from wine as he entered. Men looked at him, for he was well-known there, and indeed he had been in the *Oquendo* coming from Cholula, and I knew him. He was one of Lansons & Grailes, big shipping people.

"Hallo, Birt," he called to a man near me. "I've been dining with the President. He's got a new champagne: don't touch it: keep to his claret. I've heard all about the war, though. Damned dirty hounds, those rebels, what?"

Birt, who was an astute-looking man, rosy and rusé, with an orchid in his buttonhole, asked, with a strong Scotch accent, what the rebels had been up to, now. The other let fly at once, not so much to Birt as to the room in general.

"Been up to?" he said. "Well, something that they may think magnificent, but it isn't war. They crept into Santa Ana and sank three torpedo-boats without warning as they lay at anchor, with their crews asleep. Damned sporting, I must say, to murder sleeping men in their beds. But they didn't get much by it, I'm glad to think, except a damned swift knock in the neck. The *Moro* sunk and all her crew captured. If the President has any sense, he'll take the prisoners from the *Moro,* try the lot of them for murder and shoot them."

"I was in Boni's just now," the old Scotchman said. "He said he wasn't so sure there were any prisoners."

"If they were all drowned, so much the better: it'll save the executioners a dirty job."

"Boni didn't think they were drowned. Boni thought the rebels had got them off."

"Not likely, when they were flying for their lives."

"Maybe no, yet a shrewd wee Italianoman, yon Boni; he's got a wheen queer ways of knowing the fact."

"Well," the man snorted, "I hope to God he's wrong this time. These damned murdering rebels ought to get what they're asking for. A thing the President's hot over is their going into Santa Ana, a place all jammed with neutral shipping, and starting a naval battle there, as though it were a damned prize-ring."

"Boni was saying that they warned all the neutrals that a state of war existed," the old Scotchman went on. "I'm not saying that that justifies rebellion, or what they did, which I only know from the papers. But when a lad wants a scrap any place in the world will suit him for a prize-ring. And as for saying that they murdered yon torpedo-wallahs in their beds, that's havers. They'd no business to be in their beds. No soldier or sailor, or business-man for that matter, can be excused for being surprised. That's the first thing a man of action has to learn."

"By God, Birt," the man said, "you talk like the liberal press. Those fellows in the torpedo-boats were these rebels' shipmates and very likely messmates and relations. It makes me sick. But I must have a drink and see to Jones."

He moved away out of the room and left the company stirred to offer inside information about the battle. "You know," a man said, "the old Charger's got it wrong about that battle in Santa Ana. The President and his friends here may be making a big mistake. Well, I'll be going home to roost." He nodded to one or two and walked out, leaving me with the feeling that here and there even in Santa Barbara there were one or two who took the side of the rebels. And from what he had said, and from what the Charger had said, I began to have other views of this naval battle. It had been a dash, of course, to try to carry off the *Almirante O'Duffy* from the very heart of the enemy's harbour; and that plan had been defeated, but some Presidential torpedo-boats had been sunk: and I knew that without these torpedo-boats the *O'Duffy* might well be unable to proceed to sea at all, and might therefore be out of action till the end of the war, for which advantage the *Moro* was not too big a price to pay.

"Ah, Tom," I thought, "your side has not had much luck; but it has all the dash and all the genius. However much of a mucker your friends will come, they'll be in the stories in the days to be. Would to God I had been with you at your end, as I might have been, if I had taken your offer."

I was wearily thinking of going to bed (I didn't expect to sleep) when Roarer Bosbury came in. "Ah, Tarlton," he said, "I was looking for you. I've just heard from Peters that you say your poor cousin has been killed. I am sorry. I was much attached to your cousin: he was often with us at one time or another. Have you had news through? How was he killed?"

"Sir," I said, "I do not know that he has been killed. I only think it. He was in the *O'Duffy,* and not likely to have been spared."

"Ah, don't lose hope," he said. "But it's wiser not to hope too much. But I was looking for you about another matter, which I can't help hoping will interest you. I've been asked by a man here if I could recommend anyone to take charge of a lorry-train, going south with machinery to the mines, starting at dawn to-morrow. You would be just the man. You would be back in a week. The lorry men are mostly Welsh miners, and a bit of a handful to keep sober: otherwise it might be a picnic, I think. If you'd like it, come with me, and I'll introduce you to Mr. Hurley."

I said I would like the job, and thanked him for his thought of me. So at one in the morning I took over the lorry-train, and at dawn started with it, and had a rough picnic for the next week with neither news nor rumours, but a continual jolting on bad roads, and a tough

gang of drivers to keep sober; plenty of land-
scape to look at, to take my thought off Tom,
and a good experience, but for the dust and the
biting things.

When I got back a week later, I heard it
said at the Club that the *Moro* had not been
torpedoed, but had struck a mine, and that
though she had been sunk, most of her people
had been saved; and that though the expedition
had not taken the *O'Duffy* it had cut out and
towed away, with singular dash, and under a
heavy fire, the store-ship *Atahualpa*, laden
with artificers' equipment of all kinds. "Ah,"
I said to myself, "the rebels have had a victory,
or at least a success then."

There had been no other fighting.

I went to the station to ask about trains to
the Santa Ana frontier. I found that while I
had been away, the railways had been "mili-
tarised"; any place within a hundred miles of
the frontier was now called "within the zone"
and forbidden to civilians.

In the Club, a man told me that a war fever
was being fostered in the Press and that probably Santa Barbara would have declared war
upon the rebels, and advanced with the Santa
Ana troops to crush them, had the army been

ready for action. "But you'll see all there is in the Press," he said. "No news really. It is all censored or doctored up."

I took up that morning's copy of *El Imparcial* and found that it was as he had said. At the foot of the first page I read the following:

"IMPORTANT SEIZURE.

"The Dutch steamer *Gry*, which put in for coal yesterday, bearing a large consignment of modern rifles and their ammunition for the rebel headquarters at El Puño, has been stopped and impounded at Santa Barbara at the request of the President of Santa Ana. These munitions had been purchased by the rebels' agents in the Republic of Monte Verde, and were designed to have a decisive influence upon the conflict. We understand that rebel agents have protested against the seizure of the ship and cargo, but undoubtedly the case is one in which the impartial tribunals of international law must be invoked. The *Gry* has been placed upon moorings in the inner harbour; her officers and crew,

pending the enquiry, have been landed
and given quarters in the naval barracks."

I read this for the first time with the feeling
that it was very rough luck on the rebels, to
have their arms impounded, and that it might
well lose them the war. When I read it through
a second time, I thought: "Why should a ship
from Monte Verde put in to Santa Barbara for
coal?" And at once I leaped to the conclusion
that the captain of the *Gry* had betrayed the
cargo for money down. In the Club bar that
evening I heard a man saying:

"Funny thing about that Dutch ship with
the munitions. Her captain cabled Rivas at
the Embassy to ask what he would pay for a
chance to impound ship and cargo. Rivas
quoted him five thousand of the best, and the
chap came up to see him and drew the cash at
Meruel before ever he sailed from Monte. Not
quite cricket, what; but a knock for the rebels."

The other man agreed that it would be a
fatal knock for the rebels. All the talk of the
bar was on those lines, that the rebels had had
a knock, and the sooner they got hanged on
sour apple-trees the sooner the world could get
back to trade.

Early the next morning, as I had nothing to do, I walked down to the water-front, to look at the ships, and to see if there were any English ships, newly in, to which I could offer my services.

As I walked there, I thought that I would take a boat and run out to look at the *Gry:* apart from her link with the rebels' cause, her name interested me, for though one of the men at the Club had said that it was a Dutch proper name, perhaps the name of her original builder and owner, it is a gipsy word meaning horse; and I was interested and wondered whether her name were a gipsy name. I had had a little to do with gipsies when I was a lad, before I went to sea.

I had better describe the harbour. It is a big lake or enclosure of water three miles long by a mile broad. The northern end (two miles long) is the outer anchorage, used solely by merchant ships. The southern end (one mile long) is the naval anchorage. The two anchorages communicate, but are fenced from each other for the most part by a big mole. Both are shut from the sea by a reef, which the old Dictator topped with a great sea-embankment of masonry, so that the easterly and north-easterly gales, which set in with great violence formerly through the gaps in the reef, are now checked.

For beauty, few things can compare with a busy tropical port. In those days, just before the war, a good many sailing vessels were in use, mostly coasting schooners, and içuna-fishers, and these moving about, with their coloured sails, gave great life to the scene. There were also a few fine sailing-ships waiting there for sugar, and these, of course, took my attention.

Near them, I perceived an old friend, whom I had not expected to see so far from home. There was no doubt whatever about her, she was the famous English tug, the *Tipton Slasher*, lying at anchor, with steam up. I knew her well, and had often been on board her: as it happened, too, she had been the tug that had towed us to sea on my first voyage in the ship, *The Shining Branch*, Liverpool to San Francisco.

"Ha, the old *Slasher*," I thought. "I wonder what brings her here."

The mate of one of the sugar barques was standing near me. I asked him, "What brings the *Slasher* here?"

"She was sold to a Monte firm," he said, "which bust. She came in with a tow a day or two past, and is for sale. She had a broom at her masthead this morning, to show it, but it isn't there now, so perhaps she's been sold."

"She's a fine tug," I said.

"She's in need of an under-water scrape," he said. "That Monte firm has let her go all to hell, the way these Barboes do."

At the inner end of the merchant shipping harbour, nearly two miles from the sea-entrance, and very close to the naval harbour, is a stretch or reach known to sailors by various nicknames: the "Condemned Cell," "The Fallen Women's Home," the "Rogue's Walk," or "Moab." In this Rogue's Walk the ships which had come down in the world were impounded. There you would see the ships laid up for any reason: the ships in the receiver's hands, their owners being bankrupt, the ships caught smuggling or pearling within the limits, the ships which couldn't pay their dues or were waiting to be sold. There were usually two or three there.

My boatman said at once, that the *Gry* was in the Rogue's Walk. Already, the ship had become a place of pilgrimage. When we came to the Rogue's Walk, a dozen little boats, full of sightseers, were lying near her, with their people gawping at her. There were three ships in the Walk at the time; the *Van Hoorn,* a big black American steamer, up for sale; the *Laramie,* a very old American ship, once famous, I believe, as a corvette in the Civil War there, and now a pathetic old crock, waiting for the knackers to break her up; and my sea-rogue, the *Gry,* nearest to the naval harbour.

My little boat, which was a gay little harbour craft, with a bright green body and a sail of blue and white stripes came up under the sterns of these three. All three were moored to buoys head and stern, with their bows pointing to the outer reef.

A couple of dingy, weary-looking negroes were in charge of the *Van Hoorn;* the *Laramie* was deserted. The shore boats hung off the *Gry,* which had some life about her. I passed under her stern and had a good look at her, and seemed to remember having seen her somewhere before.

She was a ship of an old pattern, of about 3,500 tons, built with the bold sheer and clipper bow of a sailing ship. She had a small topgallant forecastle, a short poop and a big midship section, all three painted white. Her hull and smoke-stack were green, rather in need of repainting. She had the usual short masts (masts and topmasts in one piece) one in each well, between the midship house and the superstructures. She had derricks footing to the mast coats all bowsed and topped well home to the hounds. I had the feeling that she had once been fast and had always been wet. She had once carried passengers, no doubt. She had a big skylight abaft her smoke-stack which could only serve as light to a saloon. I noticed that her chart-room abaft the bridge was large: probably all her officers berthed there. As I pulled under her stern, to get to the starboard side, I saw the words:

GRY
MONTE VIDEO

embossed on her counter.

On the starboard side, she was a different ship. They had an accommodation-ladder rigged there, with a man-of-war four-oar gig lying at the foot of it. A man-of-war coxswain was in her stern-sheets sponging off the gratings. A naval messenger stood with a naval lieutenant at the ladder-head, taking the morning air. "So they have put a guard on board her," I said to my boatman. "Yes, sir," he said. "She must have a guard, being full of things that may explode." As we pulled forward along her side, I saw that some man-of-war ratings, in undress uniform, were slowly going over her forward paintwork with scrubbers. I concluded that she would therefore have a working-party as well as a gig's crew on board, all in charge of the lieutenant.

Any ship and way of carrying on will interest a sailor. I had not had much chance of seeing the Santa Barbara Navy at work, so I looked at these fellows, and concluded that the lieutenant was a young poop-ornament and that the men were slacking. "If that is a fair sample of your style," I thought, "you'd better keep peace with Santa Ana; for the Santa Ana men jump at the word, and will shoot the whites out of your eyes before you will know there's a war." I pulled away from her and then told the boatman to lie on his oars, while I had another look.

Once again I had the feeling that I had seen her before: this time it was a certainty, though I could not quite tell where. I looked at her, and then turned over in my mind the many harbours full of ships through which I had passed. I knew from memory some hundreds of ships, of course, that I could put a name and a shape to; I had certainly not heard the name *Gry* before: yet I was sure that I had seen her. "Pull round her bows," I said. "I want to see her forward." He pulled a few quick strokes, and brought me to her starboard bow. As I looked up, I saw that her clipper-bow ended in a white, prancing horse, above which a short spike bowsprit fitted, to carry off the sheer and finish the effect of the mast-rake. "A white horse," I thought. "The gipsy *Gry* after all": and on the instant there came a vivid memory of when I had seen the ship before. It had been in the Mersey, two or three years before. I had been on the landing-stage at a midday time of high water, when the river was full of moving shipping. It was a sunny morning, and I had been watching a big freighter with an enormous deck-load of scantlings coming up the river with a list. I had been thinking how lucky she was to have brought any of the deck-load home with a list on her of that sort. As I watched her, this green *Gry* had slipped quickly past her, outward bound. I had just caught the white flash of the *Gry* upon her bows, and had wondered what it was, since so few steamers have anything like a figurehead. Now, as I looked, that scene came back so vividly, the stage, the busy ferries, the gulls hovering above the river, hardly changing their slant, yet lying on the air, and the big ships passing and hooting. "Of course, that's where I saw her," I said to myself.

Something made me wish to have a look at the white *Gry* from before all, so I pulled right forward, and looked up. The *Gry* was a half-length, reared up rampant, with open mouth and flying mane. As I paused there, looking, one of the naval ratings nipped down from the knightheads on to the tail-boards and paid out, over the bows, a south-wester secured to a length of spunyarn.

"Inglisman," he called to me in a low voice. "You bring vino? Put vino in de hat. Me give dollar one." "No hay," I said, "no got vino." "You got brandy, wisky?" he asked. "No hay," I said, "nada." "You bring, eight bells to-night?" he asked. "We give lot dollars." "Nada," I said, and pulled away, and so off towards the Mole again, wondering at the

73

F

slackness of the lieutenant, that allowed a shore boat to get under the bows in daylight and then let one of his crew traffic for alcohol within twenty yards of him. "If I were your admiral, young man," I thought, "I would skin your uniform right off you before this next eight bells."

As I slipped slowly along the line of the breakwater, which shuts off the naval from the merchant harbour, I was aware that a good deal was being done in the naval harbour. Winches were rattling, and from the columns of smoke rising in the air I surmised that ships there were getting steam. As I slipped along, I noticed a man standing on the top of the breakwater, staring into the naval harbour. At my first glance I thought that he was only one of the naval sentries; but at a second glance I knew somehow that it was Tom, and that he was there as a spy. My heart almost stood still as I stared. He was in mufti, staring through binoculars at the ships of war. It was Tom without any question; not dead, not at Puño.

I saw a naval sentry come out of his box three hundred yards down the Mole, near the city; he shouted and signed to Tom to get out

74

of that. Tom was in no great hurry: he put away his glasses, slipped down a rope ladder into a boat that waited there for him, then disengaged his ladder with a brisk twitch, shoved off, and at once settled with his boatman to sail back to the stairs.

He had not noticed me, and led my boat by thirty yards. I told my boatman to follow the boat ahead, which he did, till presently we were alongside.

"Hullo, Tom," I said.

"Hullo yourself," he said. "I've been looking for you."

We talked no more till we reached the stairs, but I took a good look at him, and saw that he had aged ten years since I last saw him: he had the "war-look," which was frequent enough in 1914, though rare later, as men became used to horrors. His companion, who wore a suit of serges, was plainly another naval officer, one of the quiet, preparing kind that works on a Staff ashore.

When our boats reached the stairs, we hopped out and shook hands. "We can't talk here," he said. "Come on to my lodgings."

We thrust through the company that always collects at the stair-heads.

"I've been mourning you as dead," I said. "I thought you'd been taken in the *O'Duffy*."

"Some of the tiffies warned us," he answered. "We were out of her when they took her."

"You've been through a good deal," I said, "by your look."

"I was in the *Moro*," he said.

"What happened?"

"She hit a mine. We lost about fifty men. But it was worth it."

"I've only seen the papers here," I said. "They aren't friendly. It seemed to me to be your day."

"We did what we meant to do: put the *O'Duffy* out of action and took the store-ship," he answered. "But that is nothing. This matter of the *Gry* is the very devil. You've seen about the *Gry*, that she has been seized, with rifle-ammunition for us?"

"Yes. And I've seen the *Gry*."

"When we're under cover, we'll talk about it," he said. "In the meantime, just keep your eyes quietly skinned, to see that we aren't being followed. We'll test it, by one or two casts back, if you don't mind."

We made one or two casts back. As far as we could make out no one was following us.

Presently we were in a deserted square, where a fountain tossed water into a gold-fish pond. In the lonely square, in the shelter of the noise of the water, I asked how he had come to Santa Barbara.

"By air and a quick car this early morning," he said. "But come on; time's precious. Besides, I'm known here and it would be well if I were not seen." He led the way out of the square into a street, and thence down a narrow, dark lane, labelled the Street of the Duke of Rivas (who was a poet). The lane was too narrow for a carriage: it looked, somehow, sinister. Tom stopped at No. 13, which is not a re-assuring number, and I did not like the look of the house, which was at a bend in the lane, and all shuttered close, with a black door of old wood. Tom opened with a latch-key, and asked me into a dark passage, which became like night when the door closed. He turned on a light.

I saw white walls with a mirror, coconut matting on a stone floor, and a stair winding up. "Come up," Tom said. "I'll lead the way."

He led me to a room on the floor above, wound back the jalousies, so that I saw a pleasant, bare, cool room, and a table with maps upon it.

"Take a seat and smoke," he said. "I've been hunting for you and feared I'd never find. I tell you, I want your help, Charles."

"You shall have it," I said. "Is it about the *Gry?*"

"Yes. She's supposed to be carrying rifle-ammunition for us. So she is. But under the rifle-ammunition, unknown to the people here and to the Captain who betrayed us, are between two and three hundred of these quick-firing Poiret guns, with a thousand tons of ammunition for them, on which we count for victory. We must have those guns and ammunition belts."

"You can't," I said. "Her fires are out and she's tied up there in the Rogue's Walk."

"Well. We've got to get her to El Puño."

"That'll be a bit of a job," I said. "I suppose you've seen her? She's got a guard on board."

"Yes. Ten men and a lieutenant."

"The lieutenant's a slacker," I said.

"Even so, it's a guard. And she's very near to the naval anchorage."

"Oh, for the good old days of the cutting-out party," I said, "when you could scupper the guards and make sail. I don't see what's to be done."

"Something's got to be done," he said. "We must get her away before they rummage her hold and find those Poirets. I've got a tug."

"Do you mean the *Tipton Slasher?*" I asked.

"Yes. She was for sale. I bought her. Luckily she has steam up, for a firm in Meruel wanted her, and she was going down the coast to-day; but I stepped in and got her. That is, of course, our agents did."

"What is her crew?"

"Her Liverpool crew."

"I did hear a word," I said, "that her bottom is grassy, and that her engines aren't sound."

"She's a bit grassy; nothing to hurt. Her engines are in good order."

"Has she good lines, that would hold the *Gry?*"

"Yes, good new lines, or almost new. She can tow the *Gry* if we can get her."

"You're lucky to get such a tug as the *Slasher,*" I said. "And more than lucky to have a Liverpool crew. Do they know the kind of job expected of them?"

"The Captain's under an obligation to our

agents," he said. "He has some sort of knowledge. He knows at least that he stands to gain a great deal if he gets the *Gry* to Puño. The others know nothing."

"Tom," I said, "suppose her captain sells you, as the *Gry's* captain sold you?"

"He may," Tom said. "He may have already sold us. Or our enemies may have discovered that we've bought her, and already taken steps about it. Somehow I have the feeling that the Captain will stick to us. But I tell you, Charles, this place is as full of our enemies as a net is full of holes. Luckily, they aren't awake to war yet, but they're waking every hour, and we've no time to waste."

It seemed to me that any wideawake agent would enquire into the purchase of the tug. Then, surely, I thought, secret service agents would know of Tom's presence there. My heart sank, but I did want to say something to cheer him.

"Well," I said, "if your tugman keeps faith, that's one great asset. Your having the *Slasher* is another very great asset. But I still don't see how you're to scupper ten Santa Barbara naval ratings without having a war with Santa Barbara, which I suppose you wish to avoid."

80

"That is the devil of it," he said, "that guard. I thought there would only be a couple of watchmen. But we daren't fight the guard."

"There wouldn't be more than two on deck at two in the morning: but still . . . you'd have to scupper them or gag them . . . or do something to them. They might well give the alarm."

"Charles," he said, "if you were faced with the problem, what would you do to get her?"

"Try to tempt the guard out of her, or make them drunk."

"How would you get drink to them?"

"By a boat under the bows. A man in her asked me for some only a minute before I saw you."

"We might drug some rum, perhaps, and drug two or three of them. These people don't take to rum though like your own dear countrymen. How would you tempt them out of her?"

"I hadn't thought," I said. "Perhaps you could forge an admiralty order."

"I haven't got one to forge. I don't see how I can get one."

"I seem to remember that in the French Revolution they got women to tempt the

81

Royalist soldiers. Could we forge a love letter to the lieutenant, making an assignation with him for midnight. That might bring him ashore with his gig's crew. In his absence, the guard might be tempted with drugged rum."

"Drugging rum's a risky business," he said. "What drug? And how much of it? And how can we get it without a doctor's prescription?"

"I should have thought we could get knock-out drops from some of the saloons in Sailor Town."

"It is two plans," he said. "It isn't simple. It means one plan for the men and another for the officer. As a matter of fact the lieutenant will be ashore to-night at the President's levée."

"How do you know?"

"I heard that there was a levée, so I went to the Residency and saw on the list that the Teniente Garcia Caldera, that is the fellow, is to be there. He and the gig's crew will be out of her. That leaves six to drug: and three of those will be teetotallers; old hard-shell water drinkers with their pensions due."

"Well," I said, "let us consider a little further. We've got two things in our favour. The lieutenant's to be ashore, and we have, by a miracle, a first-rate tug. The question is how

82

to tempt the guard of six either ashore or into insensibility. What force have you?"

"Force?" he said. "No force, and wouldn't dare use it if I had it. Whatever happens, Santa Barbara mustn't declare war on us."

"Well, but what men have you to seize the *Gry*? You'll want someone to steer her at least."

"I've got myself," he said, "and I think I've got you."

"Yes, you've got me. Who else?"

"There's Grau, the man who was in the boat with me just now, and his wife, Señora Grau. This is their house, by the way. He has been in our Embassy here this last year. You can depend on those two till hell freezes, as your Admiral says. And Señora Grau is a sailor. She can steer, yes, and take a quick cast."

"Good," I said, "we are four."

"And the tug-hands, who will keep strictly to their jobs as tug-hands."

"Couldn't we drug a pie and some rum?" I said, "and bring them off to the *Gry* as a gift from the President, after the gig has taken in the lieutenant?"

"You're all for your drugs," he said. "But it will be midnight: some of them will be turned in, and all will have had their suppers. You can drug all the pies and all the wine in Christendom, but you can't be sure that you will make the crew eat and drink of them. Then these knock-out drops that you speak of are very uncertain (from what I have heard) and have been known to kill men. And anyhow, I loathe the thought of poison."

"I do, too," I said. "But we're considering possible ways of breaking all laws, and poison is one of them. However, let us consider every other way first. I should think we could go aboard at midnight, lure the man at the gangway (there isn't likely to be more than one) into a cabin, and lock him in, and then turn the key on the rest, who will probably be asleep."

"Yes, and suppose we found them all on deck?" he objected.

"We could say we brought orders that the *Gry* is to shift her berth."

"Yes, but I've reason to believe, and so has Grau, that they will shift her this afternoon right into the naval harbour: they wouldn't shift her twice in one day. Then, you must remember that the President's levée will keep both harbours full of boats almost all night long: officers will be going in sober and coming back more or less drunk all the time. There'll be a lot of traffic. We shall be under observation."

"I'm not so sure of that," I said. "There'll be thick haze in this harbour to-night."

"I never thought of that," he said. "Fog on the top of everything. There may not be fog. Who says there'll be fog?"

"I do. And this weather bureau says so."

"That settles it, then, I suppose. The tug wouldn't find her in fog and, even if she did, wouldn't be able to take her out."

"If the Liverpool crowd is in the *Slasher*," I said, "they could find her in any kind of a fog, if they would consent to try. As for taking her out, if you would trust me, I'd risk it, and do my best."

"I know you're a pukka pilot," he said, "but what chance would you have of taking her out in a fog, through a crowded anchorage?"

"A sporting chance," I said. "That's good enough."

"I suppose it's a yard-arm crime," he said. "And a yard-arm crime won't make you popular with Green & Silvers. It is piracy, isn't it, to take a ship?"

"We haven't taken her yet," I said. "How are we to take her?"

"Yes," he said. "How are we to take her?"

"Well, I've suggested that we rush her at midnight, lock the sleepers into their fo'c's'le and carry her off."

"I've objected," he said, "that we may find them all on deck, get into conflict with them, insult their flag, and give Santa Barbara pretext for declaring war. That we have to avoid at all costs."

"I suppose you would beat the Santa Barbara Navy?" I said.

"Please God, we don't have to try," he answered. "They've an army as well as a navy, with fifty heavy howitzers."

"Wait one moment," I said. "Another thing has occurred to me. I've been away for some days, and a lot has taken place here since I went. They've begun to talk of war with you. Have they established a special night harbour guard yet?"

"There are the usual harbour-police," he said. "They will take some passing. They've not mounted a special night guard yet. But the devil of it is that they may at any moment. Grau raised that very point. We must try to lift her to-night, or it may be never."

Señora Grau came into the room: I was presented to her. I liked her look of calm, resolute beauty.

"So you still seek a way?" she said.

"Yes," Tom said, "and we don't find one."

"We may get to it by elimination," I said. "It can't be done by force."

"Nor by kindness," he said.

"It will have to be done by craft or luck," I said.

"I don't see the craft; and the luck's out," Tom said.

"If I were you," Señora Grau said, "I would put it all quite out of your minds. Walk out on the front and in the plazas for half an hour, and then come back to lunch. Don't try to think of anything: something may be given."

"That is very sound advice," I said. "Let's take it."

So Tom and I walked out, and looked again at the harbour. There were the ships in their mooring-lines: there was the busy beautiful harbour, with the *Gry* on the one hand and the *Slasher* on the other. How we were to bring them together was not yet clear. I saw the steam picket-boats of the harbour-police dashing about on duty. How we could take the *Gry* out of harbour without challenge from a police-boat I could not imagine. "If there were fog," I thought, "I could take her out and ignore their challenges. Then a puff of wind would lift the fog, and the police would wireless the forts and the fleet, and the forts would shell us till the destroyers caught us; and away we should all go to the Mines for a term of hard labour."

But I turned again from this depressing thought to the more depressing thought: "You can't get the *Gry* off her moorings until you've settled her guard; and how can you settle her guard? She will have at least six hefty seamen on board, up to all the dodges in the Service, and proof against all the temptations."

Well, the more I thought of it, the gloomier I became. We wandered on from the front into the Gardens, both of us silent and perplexed with the effort to see a way where no way showed.

"It is just like butting your head against a brick wall in whichever way you turn," Tom said.

"It's like a tale I once read," I said, "of a traveller who came to a wall, which he couldn't climb, nor get through, nor get under."

"What did he do?" Tom said.

"Well, he tried all the ways, and then gave it up and went to sleep; and in the morning it wasn't there."

"Some wall, and some world," Tom said.

As we talked thus we came out of the gardens into what is called the Place of Liberty. At the northern end of this place is a fine, white stone building, known, then, as the Naval and Military Club. Over its entrance there was, then, a big bold bas-relief of the Battle for Independence, in which Almirante Browne fought a Spanish squadron just outside the harbour. Neither one of us thought that we were likely to find inspiration there, but we saw the ships in the bas-relief, and, of course, as sailors we stopped instinctively to look at them and to criticise the cuts of their topsails. On the instant, as we stopped to look, the double doors under the bas-relief were opened outwards simultaneously by two negroes in white, who held the doors wide, stiffened to attention and saluted. A moment later the cause of this salute appeared slowly walking with pomp (and some difficulty) out of the porch and down the steps.

He was a man so swathed in uniform that he looked like a tailor's dummy. He was a biggish, fat man, with a fat grey face and grey hair. On his head he wore a big black plush tricorne heavy with gold lace. He wore a naval uniform, based perhaps on what had been English practice thirty years before, but bottle-green in colour, wherever there was no gold lace. I knew how costly gold lace is, from having had to ship some in Green & Silvers. This man wore so much that he had only to be melted down to pay the national debt. He was stiff with it, epaulettes, stock, aiguillettes, rank stripes, pipings, cuff and skirt flaps, and the seams of his trousers. His sword seemed to be of solid gold: he had even a kind of gold spat which came down over each shoe, and a gold trouser strap beneath the shoe. He walked stiffly, and from instinct guessing that he must be a kind of super Admiral we both saluted him, which grace he returned with pomp. He walked slowly across the Plaza to the Admiralty. On his way, about one-third of the men whom he passed, stiffened to attention and saluted. I watched him, till the naval ratings had closed the Admiralty doors upon him.

"Who is that?" I asked. "A saviour of his country?"

"Port-Admiral here," Tom answered, "Ribeira y Pelote; an old family: they grow sugar, I believe, out to the north somewhere."

I did not answer for a few minutes, then at last I said, "Tom, come to some quiet garden where we can talk; I believe that I know how we can take the *Gry*."

We went into a lonely public garden at the back of a nunnery, and there I told Tom what I thought.

"If you will ship enough gold lace, Tom," I said, "you can go alongside the *Gry* with your tug at any hour of the day or night and take her wherever you choose."

"I don't see how," he said.

"You have seen how. You saw the Port-Admiral just now drawing salutes out of deaf-mutes. Disciplined men obey the symbol of authority, long after authority has ceased."

"Then you want me to put on a uniform of that sort, go on board the *Gry* and order them to unmoor."

"Yes."

"I believe it might work."

"I feel sure it will."

91

"That would be perfect," he said. "The English tug is a difficulty. What would a naval officer here be doing with an English tug?"

"I don't know," I said. "And they won't know, but they won't ask. 'Theirs not to reason why. Theirs but to do or die.' Like disciplined men, they will obey orders, without question."

"Yes," he said, "but as I told you, they will have shifted the *Gry* during the afternoon. This second shift, with an English tug, will be more than they'll swallow."

"They'll swallow any order backed by enough gold lace. If you ship enough stripes, you can take a new crew from the guard-house, and put all the *Gry's* present crew under arrest."

"That is an idea," he said.

"You bet it's an idea."

He seemed to be inclined to accept the plan.

"It depends on one thing," I said. "Can you get a uniform like that Port-Admiral's?"

"Something like it, perhaps, but I'm not sure, because it's the President's levée to-night; all the outfitters with levée dress-uniforms to hire will have hired theirs out by this time."

"Could you buy one?"

"I might be able to buy one second-hand, or from the theatre-people."

"Go out and try it," I said. "If you get it, put it on to-night, go boldly down to the Naval Stairs, order a guard to take you in a picket boat to the *Gry*; assume command of her, put her crew under arrest, make them unmoor her for you; the *Slasher* will then appear; you can send all the naval men ashore in the picket-boat, and proceed to sea."

"It's a scheme," he said.

"You bet it's a scheme."

"One point I should change," he said. "We ought to go in the boat to the *Slasher* and have the *Slasher* with us when we reach the *Gry*. Then we could start at once."

"The sooner the better," I said.

"Even so, there'll be the police-patrols at the harbour-mouth. How are we to get past them?"

"Don't you think we might bluff the police-patrol with gold lace, if we can bluff the naval ratings?"

"We might," he said, "but the *Gry* is a marked ship; a prisoner in fact. They will ask what is this prisoner doing out of prison."

93

"We can say that we're taking her to Cape Catoche for greater safety."

"They'll ask for the Admiralty orders."

"Forge some."

"So you said before. I would if I had the forms, but I haven't, and don't know what they look like, and haven't time to find out."

"Will you try the plan?" I asked. "Will you buy a uniform?"

"I'll try to," he said. "It is the only likely plan propounded so far. I'll have to buy two uniforms: one, of lesser rank, for Grau. As I don't want to be recognised, would you try to buy the uniforms?"

"But they'd know me for an Englishman. They'd never sell them to me. And I should not know the things to ask for."

"True," he said. "I must do it. I daren't risk going to the outfitters. I shall go to a theatrical costumier's down near the Front. I'll have to buy: there'll be none left for hire."

The costume-shop near the Front had a bright window, in which a bottle-green naval uniform, thick with gold lace, fronted a sky-blue soldier's uniform, thick with silver lace. In between them, a wooden ballet-girl in spangles stood archly on one leg. I told Tom

94

that he had better go in alone, and to this he agreed.

After he had gone in, I hung about on the Front, looking at the harbour. The taking of the *Gry* was still far off in the future. The event of the moment was the getting of the uniforms.

I have always hated the cocksure man and dreaded any feeling of confident certainty when about to attempt anything. When there is a sort of hopeful distrust, a mixture of resolve and dread, then the soul wins helpers who will often bring her through. I was afraid that Tom was too confident that the uniform would be supplied.

I tried to think what a London or Portsmouth outfitter would do, if asked for such a uniform. They would ask for the name and consult the Navy List. "If they do that here," I thought, "and Tom gives a false name, the chances are, either that the name won't be in the List, or that the man whose name he gives will be known to them: he may, even, be one of their clients."

Then I thought, the police here must be on the look-out for gate-crashers at the levée. They must always be trying to prevent impersonation, or people coming into the Presidency under false colours. They will have some understanding with the outfitters no doubt, so that they may learn beforehand what uniforms have been issued. Even if this be not London or Portsmouth, but a city in the sun, it is in a state of unrest, with a beginning war-fever; precautions must be growing more stringent hourly.

I walked up and down, wondering why Tom didn't come out; ten minutes passed, the quarter hour passed. I began to be very anxious, thinking that he must have been arrested, or held during enquiries. I imagined the tailor being bland and suave, trying the fit of this or that, while his colleague in the back shop telephoned to the secret police to send a man to make enquiries. After I had been waiting for twenty minutes a car drove up to the door of the outfitters. Two men, who looked very like police-officers, came out of the car, entered the shop and remained there.

Ten more minutes passed.

I had given up hope almost, when Tom suddenly appeared, followed by a boy carrying a tin uniform case. A taxi-cab drove up, the boy opened the door for Tom, put in the case, received a tip and went. The cab drove off, passed me, turned a corner, and then stopped for me. We drove for a couple of hundred yards without speaking, because in those southern parts there is no partition between driver and passenger. Tom stopped the car and dismissed it. When we were in one of the public gardens, sure that we were not being followed, Tom said, "I have the uniform complete."

"I thought you'd been arrested," I said. "You've been there for hours."

"Was I?" he said. "It didn't seem long. There were two or three little things to be done to the suit, and I had to try quite a lot of boots and hats."

"Were no questions asked?"

"Questions? No. Those fellows are second-hand men, only too glad of a sale."

"We're over the fence, then?"

"Over that fence, probably; yes. It never was a fence."

"It was to me," I said.

"Ah, no," he answered, "the real fence is there, out there to the left, that low yellow building on Nun's Point. That's the Harbour Police Station; and how we're to get past that unchallenged I do not see. Whatever bluff we throw will be called there."

"All right, Tom," I said. "I'll take her out through Drake's Entrance, where the police won't be."

"Drake's Entrance?" he said. "Do you mean over there?"

"Yes. There, where the water's breaking."

"But there's no passage there."

"Drake got through."

"Yes, Drake in his little ships. There's not enough water for the *Gry*."

"Yes, there is," I said.

"But, good Lord," he answered. "It's a blind passage all sown with rocks, and it isn't lit and isn't even buoyed. No one uses it."

"It's well charted. I've read the chart."

"Yes, but what good will the chart be? You will be in a tug with a tow in perhaps blind fog, groping like the blind. What will guide you, when you're in it?"

"The lead," I said. "And then there are two spouting rocks, which make an odd noise. And there are bell-buoys on the worst shelves. And at the entrance one can get an echo."

"Those are only sounds, when all is said," he answered. "It's the devil of a place."

"There's a chart in the shelter there," I said. "Come down and look at it. It isn't so bad, believe me."

On the sea front at that time, there were various kiosks, or shrines, to the memory of famous men. Some of them had large scale charts of the harbour on their walls, so that visitors might pick out the various points and at night identify the beacons. I led the way to the nearest kiosk, and ran my finger along the course of the Drake's Channel. I was right: there was plenty of water for the *Gry*, but only in a narrow twisting lane. In that lane the shelves thrust into the channel in a way that cooled my ardour. The chart was printed in tints of blue to show the different depths of water, from the ultramarine of the ocean to the palest tinge, almost a white of the shore. The channel had at all times a steady five fathoms on it, often deepening to seven, but it curved like a reversed S laid on its side, thus: ᘓ and its bends were narrow. It was at the bends that the sides shoaled. Tom was right about there being no light upon it. There were two bell-buoys at ugly points, and a beacon on each of the two rocky islets at the mouth of it to seaward. These would be invisible or almost invisible to vessels coming out. Of other guides to the mariner groping out, the only ones likely to be useful were the two blowing holes, one at each bight of the S, the East and West Roarers. Two blowing holes, which might not be always blowing, and two bell-buoys, which perhaps one could not depend upon, made but slight comfort to one in a narrow channel, towing, in fog. Still, it might not be foggy; we should avoid the police that way; and then I was young and fancied my skill. Besides, the sun was shining as though it could never be night, and my friend was there, as though it could never be foggy. It was only taking a ship round a bend, and then round another bend, and then round a corner; who couldn't do that, or, at least, who wouldn't try?

"You see," I said, "there's water enough. With a good quick leadsman you could do it blindfold."

"Blindfold," he repeated. "On a clear moonlit night with no wind, you might scrape through, with luck, but to-night, in a fog, with a tow, you'll pile her up and leave her bones there. No man could take a ship through that in fog."

Even as we spoke, a man entered the kiosk and posted up the mid-day Meteorological Report, which promised very fine hot weather with haze or fog along the coast at night.

"Blindfold," he repeated, jerking his hand at the report. "Put it out of your head. You can't think of it."

We went out of the kiosk and looked at that distant naval harbour, and the sea beyond it. At the moment, what with the wind and the set of the tide the reefs in Drake's Entrance were breaking white, and the Roarers spouting. Far out to sea, as it seemed, at what was the very mouth of the entrance, the two rocky islets flashed with spray.

Seen from a distance like that, when all the teeth were showing, I must say it looked "the devil of a place" that Tom called it.

"So you won't try it?" I said.

"No," he said, "it's out of the question. Let's lunch."

"Let us lunch well," I said, "for we may not lunch well again for some time."

"Let us call for the Graus," he said.

We drove back to Duke of Rivas Street, and went to the big bare room. The two Graus came in. Grau was a sturdy stocky seaman,

with a scar on his jaw, where an Indian had
jabbed him with a spear: it gave him a kind of
hesitation in speaking. Both the Graus looked
perturbed.

"Have you heard the news while you've
been out?" Grau asked.

"No; no new news," we said. "What is it?
Fighting?"

"No," he said. "But the harbour is to be
closed to-night with a boom."

"Whatever for?"

"A measure of precaution, they say. There's
no doubt of it. I went out to make sure: and
they've got it half-rigged already. There'll be
no taking out the *Gry* by that way."

"Are they closing Drake's Entrance, too?"
I asked.

"What is Drake's Entrance?"

"The southern channel," I said.

"I didn't know that there was a southern
channel. Do you mean among all those reefs?"

"Yes."

"If it be a channel, I suppose they'll close it,
but I shouldn't think that anyone would try
to take a ship there. It isn't buoyed, nor lit."

"Have you charts handy?" I asked.

"Charts and to spare," he said. Charts were

102

brought and unrolled. I gazed at them, and as I gazed, I thought of old Drake, and felt oddly that he was near and ready for a flutter. That winding serpent of the channel became luminous in my mind. "I can master you," I thought, "though Scylla barks there and Charybdis bites here, and the rocks rise up and clash at me."

Grau looked over my shoulder as I looked at the charts.

"Drake's Entrance looks like a pretty rocky alley," he said.

"It's all that," I answered, "but you've got a Liverpool tug with all her crew. Any Liverpool tug-master would try it."

"In thick weather?" Grau said. "It will be thick to-night."

"It's thick in the Mersey one day in four," I said, "they don't stop for thickness."

"Perhaps not," Tom said, "but they know the Mersey. They don't know this place."

"I know it pretty well," I said.

"Well, it seems the only thing left," Grau said. "So, you countryman of Drake, what do you advise us?"

"I should say, let's go aboard the tug and get the tug-master to come with us, in a motor-boat, to see Drake's Channel. If he says it can't be done, be sure it can't be done. If he says he'll try it then you may be sure that there's a chance."

"Very good," Tom said, "we'll put it to the tug-master."

"I'll take a chart or two," I said, "and a compass if you've got one."

"I've a boat compass," Grau said, "it isn't what you call great shakes."

"Well, it will serve," I said, "while we go round the bends with it."

"It would be as well," Grau said, in his hesitating way, "if we didn't show the charts. They may have sentries on the sea wall. We'd better seem to be fishing. I'll take lines. In this last day or two, these people have been a bit spy-mad."

We put the charts into a dispatch case; Grau pocketed the compass, and took two wooden frames of sea-line with spoon bait. At the Stairs we hired a motor-boat, the *Galfrido*, in which we put out, through the small craft, to the *Slasher*.

I had so often seen the *Slasher* in old days in the Mersey. She had been in the talk of seamen for years, for many famous tows. On one day that was memorable to myself I had seen

her lying close alongside the *Shining Branch,*
ready to take us to sea: and had envied her men
with their breakfast of kippers while I, as a
reefer, breakfasted on an outward-bounder's
bread. There she was again, a part of the
Mersey, in that far away port, a piece of England in that foreign place: one of the picked
tugs of the world, giving that sense of quiet
power which takes a sailor's eye.

"What is her Master's name?" I asked. "It
used to be Stott."

"Stott is dead," Tom answered. "Her present man is Tollick. Julius Cæsar Tollick."

"That's an odd name," I said.

"He's an odd man, perhaps," Tom said.
"But more than precious to me at this time."

The *Galfrido* ran alongside the *Slasher.* We
climbed aboard her. An alert-looking, pale-
faced man, with fair side-whiskers and a bushy
moustache, came forward to meet us. I noticed
that he gave us an extraordinarily swift sharp
scrutiny. This was Captain Tollick. There
was no doubt at all of his being a resolute soul
with a quick intelligence. I did not doubt that
he was by nature a dare-devil who would
gamble on a chance. Tom introduced us. The
Captain led the way to his little cabin and

105

offered us whisky and white Peru brandy, which we refused. Tom explained that the main entrance was to be closed, and that the other would be our only chance. "It's a bad, narrow, twisting channel," he said, "and it will be foggy, or at least thick, from midnight on."

The Captain looked at him, then at Grau and myself.

"Do any of you know this channel?" he asked.

"I've got a general hang of it," I said.

"Is there water for this ship?"

"Yes, at any state of the tide."

"What is the set of the tide?"

"Going out on a flood, it would come dead ahead in the narrowest bit. In the second and third reaches the reefs would kill the set, but you would get it ahead again as you turned for open water." He nodded and asked:

"What speed tide would you get, sir?"

"I don't know," I said. "It will be on the charts. But it is now just the tide we'll have after midnight. Perhaps you could come with us to have a look at the place, and see it for yourself."

"There's nothing I'd like better," he said.

"What do you think about trying this channel?" Tom asked him. "Would you be prepared to risk it?"

"I'd better see it, sir, with my own eyes, before I say. What am I likely to meet in it, sir?" (This last was to me.)

"Rocks shelving down or jutting out into the fairway," I said.

"I don't mean that, sir," he said. "Shall I find ships put in to anchor, or fishing-boats with their nets down, or some coastwise steamer clawing in in the fog, and then have to alter course suddenly?"

"As far as I know, the channel is never used," I said. "Fishers go there, of course. You might meet them; but you won't find ships moving or anchored there. Isn't that right?" I asked Grau.

"It's not a fairway," Grau said.

"The old Dictator was going to make it one," Tom said, "but it would cost seven million and the present men shrink from it."

Captain Tollick thought for half a minute. "Have you a picture of it?" he said, meaning a chart.

We spread a chart for him: he looked at it with keen attention for perhaps twenty seconds. I noticed that he measured the distance of each reach with his forefinger.

"What do you think of it?" Tom asked.

"We'd better have a look at it, sir," he said cheerfully. "It's best to know these places like the palm of your hand. I'll get my mate, Harry, to come, too, sir, if you've no objection. And no time like the present."

"I can give you the exact course and distance of each reach," I said. "And I'll have time to work out what you'll have to allow for sets and currents. There'll be no wind."

"Let's look at it, sir," he said; "seeing is believing, but feeling hath no fellow." He opened the door to us, we went out on to the deck. "Harry," he called, "just put on a shore hat and come along for a spot of fishing with these gents."

The mate, "Harry," I never knew his other name, all hands called him Harry, came up with his hard hat. He was a short, very powerfully built man, with the brightest eyes I have ever seen in any human head. They did not glow, as Burns's eyes were said to have glowed, they glittered. He had a deep sea-voice, and a roll in his walk; from him came a hot, sweet reek of Navy Plug chewing tobacco. He had blue roses skilfully tattooed upon the backs of his hands. I had not felt quite at ease about Captain Tollick: there was something nervy and restless about him. (I have thought since then that these qualities were only in myself.) But Harry at once reminded me of Sir Francis Drake. That short compact figure, all readiness and force and humorous courage, was just as Drake's. "This is Drake come back," I said to myself, "to take us out by this channel."

When we were in the motor-boat, threading through the shipping on our way to the channel, I told him that Drake had come that way, towing with the ship's boats ahead. "My old grandmother," he said, "she's got an old book written by one of her people who was with Sir Francis Drake. It's a little book, written in the old writing. I can't read it myself, but it's all about this Barbaro as he calls it."

Presently, we were past the *Gry*, where the sightseers still loitered in their pleasure-boats. We neared the entrance to the naval harbour. Tollick turned to Tom. "Are you quite sure, sir," he asked, "that they're not going to put a boom down here?"

"I'm not at all sure," Tom said. "The chances are that they will. They haven't yet."

"If you want to stop a bottle," Tollick said, "a cork in the mouth's the best ever: that's sure. They've got no gear for it yet though."

The marine sentry on the sea-wall moved a few paces towards us to see us go in. To divert him, I began to clear the fishing lines. We ran through the entrance into the naval harbour, and past some old hulks in use as storeships. Two cables further on we stopped with our bows to seaward exactly opposite the entrance to Drake's Channel.

The entrance lay between two moles or sea-walls, each with a beacon upon it. The space between these walls was perhaps 110 yards across. That was the gate through which the *Gry* would have to go.

"And suppose they put a boom down there?" said Tollick. Tom shrugged his shoulders.

We all stared at that bright gate. The tide was making; a small set of ripple and bubble was coming in upon us through it, slapping at our bows, making us dance a little, and driving past us, further into the dock, the muck floating there, of corks, straw, packing-case wood, a bottle or two, and (as I noticed) some cut flowers.

I lifted my eyes past these: we were all staring intently: we saw ahead of us, far out, the line of water lifted, as it seemed, a foot or two above the level of the sea. It kept trembling there. There was one visible rock there; the line of lifted water marked the reef on both sides of it.

"That's the first turn," I said, pointing to the rock. "If you enter her plumb in the middle and keep her straight, she is fairly safe in this reach. Can you trust your compass?"

"The compass is O.K.," he said. "Let's go into it and have a look."

We forged slowly ahead against the bubble of the incoming water. Soon we were passing between the beacons, which rose up, one on each side, topped by iron lanterns in shape not unlike those on the sterns of old wooden men-of-war.

When I had looked at it from the gardens in the city a couple of hours before the set of the tide had made the reefs show their teeth. Now most of the reefs were covered, and, except for some whiteness on my right, the water was still, with a few birds sleeping on it or cruising. As I watched my course, I saw a white column rise out of the sea ahead. It went

111

up leisurely against the sky, seemed to spread itself and pause and flash and fall. After a few seconds the blast of it reached us, a melancholy noise like a whale's blowing. It was the East Roarer, one of the few things I should have to guide me.

Tom and Grau dropped their lines overboard, but I know they watched that water as anxiously as I did. We went slowly on towards the East Roarer, on a course of east by north. The water is exquisitely clear there, so clear that I could see on both sides of me the rocky walls of the channel, almost like the banks of a gorge, all beautiful with scarlet coral, and dazzling white shells. I could see fish floating and gulping or flashing away with a quick fin; and I thought to myself: "Charles Tarlton, if you don't watch your tip, those fish may be nibbling you before to-morrow morning."

I suppose that all anxious people will snatch at whatever seems like a favourable omen. As we entered the channel I saw on a rock ahead some of the rather rare Alfarero birds. They rose up as we drew near and skimmed away to another rock, where they ran and splashed in the shallow pools after the small fry upon which they live. They are birds of great beauty and speed, blue in head and body, with long white swallow tails. They are not often seen now, but I pointed them out to Tom as birds of good omen. "You see," I said, "they wear the Puros colours."

The middle of that reach is rather uncomfortably narrow.

"You see, Captain," I said, "the sides of this channel draw in like a tightened sleeve there."

"I was thinking that," he said, sucking in his lips. "Can you trust your picture?"

"I expect they've got everything marked on it accurately," I said. "It is only ten years old."

"Well, the rocks won't shift much, that's sure," he said. "Rocks on both sides and small corals below: and the course dead straight for the roaring rock." He turned to Harry, who was intent upon the reach. They talked together in low voices, about revs and lengths. I kept away from them, so that they might be undisturbed. I noticed, then, that the incoming run of water made odd shadows run like water-snakes along the rocks on each side, a little below the surface. These shadows seemed ominous to me till I saw what they were.

We stole quietly on, Tom and Grau pretending to fish, but with an eye to everything. We others watched the narrow channel, and the immense, whitish, greenish or gaily coloured rocks of the under-water reefs on both sides of us. Dark alleys of water led into these here and there, all so clear that one could see tendrils in them, like floating plants, suddenly change shape and leap as the tendrils caught their prey.

I had tried to find a rhythm in the spout of the Roarer: there was no rhythm: he only spouted when the water struck with the right pressure, at irregular times.

"Can we count on that rock spouting, sir?" Tollick asked me.

"When the tide's coming in, as it will be to-night," I said.

"That'll be as good as a bell-buoy," Harry said. I didn't think it would be, myself.

We now came to the bend in the channel quite close to the East Roarer rock.

"Let's take a turn or two about here, sir," Tollick said. "You'll get some fish under this rock."

"I'd make it just under forty-three to this place," Harry said. I think that he had reckoned the distance of the first reach by lengths of the *Slasher*.

"There'll be eddies and a set here," Tollick

said. He made us take a turn or two about that bend in the reach. There was undoubtedly a set towards the reef on our right, and in that narrow place, with so little room to get the towed ship round the corner, a set might make all the difference.

"It won't be worse than it is now," Tollick said. "What does the picture say of it?"

"It doesn't mention the set of the tide," I said.

"And this is where we turn?"

"Yes, this is the first turn: you'll have to alter course seven points to starboard here. Not much room, is there?"

"None too much, I'd say."

"Shall we go on?" I asked.

"Shove ahead," he said.

The launchee took his remark to mean Full Speed Ahead. Tollick checked him with his hand. "Go slow, son, please," he said. "You see" (he added, turning to me), "we've the sun in our eyes here. Go very slow. I don't like the look of that, sir."

"What? You mean the sand?"

Out to seaward from us, on the great barrier reef that shut us from the ocean, a sand-bank had been pushed up in the course of time.

115

There was white water lipping round it, and then lipping on, creaming and whitening, over the submerged rocks into the channel.

"Does your picture mention sand, sir?" Tollick asked. "As anywhere in the reach?"

"No, no sand in the channel."

"Well, there is sand, there, just on ahead," he said. "It's been scoured right over into the fairway, no doubt, in these last few years. What depth does the picture give just there, sir?"

"Five fathoms," I said. "It's the shallowest patch on this reach."

"Well, you've not got it, sir. I know the colours of water. You've not got five fathoms there, nor near. Harry," he called, "there's a nigger in the 'simmon patch. Get a sinker on your line and try the water here."

Harry unbent the hook from his line, bent, instead, a boat's iron crutch to it, and plumbed the depth. Hauling swiftly in, he measured it off across his chest, and said, "Four of me, which makes twenty-one foot four, and by the look of it she's shoaling."

Tollick sucked his lip, while the mate made another cast. She was shoaling. A bank of sand had been piled over or through the reef to shelve half across the reach.

"And that's not in the picture," Tollick said.

"No mention of it here," I said.

"They were blasting on the outer reef," Grau said, "in the last of the Dictator's days: they probably opened up a way for a current to set the sand in."

"Well, it's here now," I said. "We must see what it amounts to. Carry on with the fishing, meanwhile."

As it happened, the fish were busy at that point where the seepings of the tide ran: they bit well, as we got the bearings and dimensions of the bank. It was roughly eighty yards long by thirty broad, running to a ridge (we judged) well in the centre of the channel. It reduced the fairway to less than eighty yards at that stretch of the reach.

"Just as well we had a look-see," Tollick said, "instead of trusting to the picture. We'd have piled her up nicely on to that lot. We'll go to the end of this reach and then back again, slowly, so as to have the sun behind us."

We slipped on towards the next bend, which is known as the Crook. Just at the bend, they had fixed a bell-buoy.

I suppose the bagpipe is a melancholy music

to most Englishmen, but a thousand bagpipes couldn't be as doleful as a bell-buoy. There was this melancholy bird in its cage rocking out its crawling clang. The buoy marked the starboard side of the turn. The port side of the channel was not marked in any way at that point, it was just left for ships to avoid or to find out for themselves. It was not breaking water, but one could see the sea a paler green there, and guess what lay beneath.

We went to the bell-buoy, then cruised back, watching the water. We found no other shoals. Such casts as we took confirmed the depths given on the chart. Tollick and Harry seemed to work together at the job before them like a mason's two hands.

We were not alone in the reach when we turned again towards the sun: three gay fishing-boats came running in to fish upon the bank. I was afraid at first that they might be naval picket-boats come to question us. I was getting into such a state at that time that I saw a naval spy or secret service man in every mortal within a mile. On a signal from Tollick we returned again to the Crook, where the turn was something a little sharper than a right-angle.

"See the jobble," Harry said, nodding at the water in front.

The "jobble" was a four-knot stream running diagonally into the water ahead. It set in from the sea-reef, and being troubled, though not broken, it was much darker than the rest of the reach.

"That'll bring her head round," Tollick said.

To me, who looked at it from the boat, it seemed likely to bring her broadside round and pile her on the bell-buoy opposite.

We turned round the Crook directly into this jobble, so that our men might test its strength. It tossed the boat about like a cork, though it did not set us to the bell-buoy as I had expected.

Just beyond the Crook, the channel narrowed, to what is called on the charts the Boneyard. I should say that it deserves its name. When in the Boneyard we had the West Roarer, that guide to shipping, dead ahead.

"Hold on with the boat," I said to the launchee, "I want to watch the spouting rock there."

We held off and fished while I watched the Roarer. It is a lump of rounded rock rising well above the surface, about the size of a tennis court and the height of an elephant. The sea has worked its way into it in the course of ages, and gets well inside it and slaps and gurgles there in the hollow place. Then from time to time some running wave fills her, spouts and leaps aloft from the blow-pipes with a shrill hissing noise, followed by a sharp "grumph," quite unlike the noise of the East Roarer, even if two of the three pipes fail. The charts said that there were two spouts; I saw three; and on asking the boatman, he said that the third had opened recently and that others would come in time, as the sea was always working there, inside.

Harry said that it would be better than nothing, and that the flash of the spouts might be useful.

Tollick pointed to a rip-raps in the mid-channel just off this West Roarer. "Looks like another sand-bank that isn't in the picture," he said.

On going into it, we found that it was not that, but a patch of confused water caused at that state of the tide by the jobble mentioned above running into the inset from the open sea.

"Is this our last turn?" Tollick asked.

"Yes," I said. "Alter course here twelve points to the eastward for the open water."

"And a good broad channel, too," Tollick said. "Room to breathe again."

I thought to myself, that that patch of confused water, where a tow would be steadied down to get her round the bend, would be just the place for her to take a sheer and go smash into the West Roarer.

On our right hand there, a great underwater reef trended away to the south. It was either a dark coral, or rock covered with a growth to a bright claret colour. The reef is called Snapper Reef, from the fish that can be had there.

Away on our left hand was another reef called the Stella Maris reef, from a ship that was once lost upon it. There is a bell-buoy where the ship struck. This reef breaks the water here and there: it is an ugly place in a sea.

"So those are all the flowers in the nosegay?" Tollick said.

"Yes. That's the lot," I said. "From here it's a clear course all the way."

"And deep?"

"Seven fathoms, deepening to twelve."

"Right," Tollick said. "We'll go back the way we came."

A good many little fishing-boats with gaily coloured sails stood into the channel between the islets as we turned for home.

"They'll be fishing here to-night," Tollick said. "We'll have to look out for those fellows."

When we were back at the sandbank I did some sounding, to find out if the lead would give us warning of it as we drew near. I found that it rose up so steeply that a ship might get a half four, yet be stuck in the sand before the sounder could make another cast. Then its hump did narrow the channel, to about seventy yards. There wouldn't be much margin for a passing ship there.

"A block in the traffic," I said.

"We'll have to go round it, sir," Harry said.

"A tightish fit," I said.

"Ah, it's nothing," he answered. "We take these things as they come."

As we returned, we noticed a party of men in undress naval uniforms at work at pully-hauly on the Mole.

"There they are," Tom said. "They're going to close the naval harbour. Those chaps are man-handling a boom."

"It looks like it."

"They're only assembling the gear for it," I said. "They're not quick doers in this fleet."

"All the life stopped in this land, when the old man died," Tollick said.

As we passed from the naval to the outer harbour, we saw that the men were in fact preparing a boom. They had some old spare spars afloat there: they were also rigging tackles by which to haul them across the entrance. "That'll be closed by sunset," Grau said, "which looks like a stopper over all, as you say."

"It's far from being rigged yet," I said. "Don't call the door shut till you find it bolted." They weren't doing it with much sense, as it seemed to me.

In a few minutes we had a more cruel shock: the *Gry* was being unmoored, two of their Admiralty tugs were plucking her out of her berth in the Rogue's Walk towards the naval harbour.

"Hold on, all," Tom said to the launchees; then turning to us he said: "They're going to

123

put her into the naval harbour, whether they shut the door or not. We'll follow the shore boats till we see what they do with her. If they berth her in with the destroyers we're done."

Several shore boats, filled with sightseers, were watching her shifted. She stole slowly forward, then straightened on her course, one tug ahead, one alongside: the boats followed her: we in the launch came with them, till we saw what was to be done with her.

She was plucked past the first and second tiers of hulks, store-ships and special-course ships, such as are in every naval harbour. In the third tier, they brought her round, head to sea, between a submarine depot-ship and a seaplane-carrier. There, instead of mooring her, they let go an anchor.

"Just for the night," Grau commented. The tugs gathered in their lines and made off to their berths. The shore-boats turned for the outer anchorage: we in the launch went with them.

I took the bearings of the entrance of Drake's Channel from the *Gry's* berth. It was N.E. ½ N.; the distance by estimation (and the chart) 650 yards.

"Back to the tug," Tom said to the launchees, "muy pronto."

On our way back, we saw them still preparing the boom. The harbours were to be shut: our chances of getting the *Gry* were dim.

When we were in Tollick's cabin, Tom said to him: "Supposing we can reach the *Gry*, what chance have you of getting her to sea through that channel?"

"I'd say a very good chance, sir."

"Even in fog?"

"Yes, sir."

"Even thick fog? I've known it dense here."

"I'd say so."

"You would be prepared to try it?"

"Yes, sir; my Mate and I would try it."

"And what is the chance? Fifty-fifty?"

"Oh, no, sir; better than that. Seventy."

"More than that, sir," Harry said, "but there's luck in these things: some amount of luck."

"Right," Tom said, "that's the chance of getting to sea. Now for the chance of getting the *Gry*. This tug will be shut into this harbour at seven to-night, unable to put to sea, by the one door or to reach the *Gry* by the other."

125

"There's only one thing that this tug can do," I said. "She must get out of this harbour before she's shut in. She'll have to put into Drake's Channel now and stay there till it's time to fetch the *Gry*."

"She'll have to get to sea," Tom said, "as though she were going to Meruel. Then, when it is dark, she could turn in by Drake's Passage, and come to the *Gry* by that."

"They may bar that, too," Grau said.

"They haven't begun to bar it yet," I said, "and it will take them hours to bar it. But I don't suppose they'll dream of barring it. They don't dream of anyone using that channel. It will be there like an unbolted back door."

"They may bar it," Grau repeated.

"They're more likely to patrol it," Tom said, "with picket-boats."

"Or a q.f. gun on the Mole," I said. The q.f. gun was the likeliest thing of all, but I was the first to suggest it. There was a kind of chill upon the talk at this point. The thought of a q.f. gun going "tackatackatacka" at us was not cheering.

"I can't get to sea, as though for Meruel," Tollick said. "To do that, I'd have to have

126

papers, and it's too late to get the papers: it's five now."

"You'll have to get into Drake's Passage, then," I said, "and keep there till we start."

"The picket-boats will board us, and the police will challenge us," he said. "What are we to say to them?"

"Say you want to do some fishing."

"That'll be a likely yarn," he said.

"But it *is* a likely yarn," I said. "We've been fishing and want to do some more. There's a police-boat coming past us now. I'll hail her."

"She's probably coming to arrest us, anyway," Grau said.

"Not a bit of it," I said. "Stay here a moment." I went on deck as the police-boat drew near. I hailed the guardias in her, and held up some fish.

"You like some fish?" I asked. They said that they would be very glad of some; so I handed down a bucketful. Then I asked if the tug might go fishing among the reefs, there and then? They looked surprised, but said: "Sure." After a pause, one of them asked: "The whole tug?" I said: "Yes." They muttered among themselves; then one said: "Of course, you can fish among the reefs, but it is dangerous: and the harbour will be shut at seven. Don't be shut out."

"Would you shoot me?" I asked.

"I don't think we'd shoot you," he said, "but you'd have to stay out all night and the reefs are bad places."

"Well, I'd like to get some fish," I said.

"Well, God has put them there," the guardia said. After that, the police-boat sheered away. I called Tom on deck to discuss things.

"There it is," I said. "Police-boat Five says that we may fish in Drake's Channel, so that is where we will go till it is time to fetch the *Gry*."

He did not seem to pay any heed: he was looking at the mail-steamer anchorage, where the launches had gathered about the Southern Mail ship.

"There's the *Garcilaso*, in from Monte," he said. "There'll be mail for Grau in her, if the spies here don't get it."

"They won't get it," I said.

"Charles," he said, "you've helped all along in this, and made all the wise suggestions. I've not really slept since the battle and can't suggest anything. But now; things aren't shaping well: there's danger. Keep out of this to-night."

"Not I," I said. "I'm in this with you. What I prompted I'll share in."

"No, no," he said. "I'm thinking of the q.f. gun on the Mole. Even if that isn't there, this business may ruin you with Green and Silvers."

"All right," I said.

"But there's nothing you can do."

"Oh, yes, there is," I answered. "And I want now to send you and Grau ashore. When you are there, send out Mrs. Grau to get a lead-and-line at a chandler's: yes, and an Indicator Log. Then get some rest. I've got things to work out here with Tollick."

"Charles," he said, "I want you not to come to-night. There's no need. Tollick and his Mate can do all there is to do."

"I know," I said. "But I suggested this, and as a pilot it interests me. I'm coming. That's final. In any case, you two must go ashore now. Later in the evening, after we've been in Drake's Channel for a while, I'll contrive to get to you somehow, to tell you if we can get to the *Gry*."

129

"What do you think about that?" he asked.

"I think that they have been great fools not to develop Drake's Channel and use it; or to realise its danger and bar it," I said. "But these people are slack and I don't believe they've thought of it. I believe that it will be an open back door."

There was some more discussion, for he was not easy to persuade, but at last he and Grau went down into the launch and away. I was left thinking that Tom was more fit for a week in bed than a night raid like ours.

When they were gone, I went at it with Tollick and the Mate for a few minutes, getting details of the channel, the courses for each reach, the exact distances of each course, the number of revolutions needed and the allowance to be made for the different sets of tide and current. While we were doing this, a boat from the agents came alongside and tossed aboard a packet of letters and papers for the tug: they had come to the port from Monte, in the *Garcilaso*, at noontime. Tollick pitched the packet into his bunk, saying that the evening was the time for letters; he wanted to be out in the channel before the booms were hauled across.

Going on deck, he got the tug under way, and as she moved slowly towards the naval harbour, he told his deck-hands to rouse out all their fishing-gear.

As they had been for a year or so in waters full of fish they roused out a good display.

I had now taken the plunge: I was one of a crew conspiring to commit an act of piracy, which, as Tom said, is "a yard-arm crime." I didn't feel any wickeder than usual, in fact, I felt happier; I was bearing a hand for Tom in the hour of his need.

All the same, as we drew near to the naval harbour entrance I became exceedingly anxious. They had not yet barred the way, but the boom was ready or nearly ready: and the gear was all rigged for hauling it across. Gangs of men were at work upon the gear on both sea walls; and naval picket-boats were there, with directing officers fussing about. Among the boats was the Harbour Police Boat No. 6 which came up to us as we drew near, and hailed us to ask where we were going.

I answered that Police Boat 5 had given us leave to go out to fish upon the reefs near-by.

"How long will you be?" he asked.

"Oh, not long," I said, "if the fish bite."

"If they bite or not," he said, "remember that this boom will close at seven. Don't be shut out for the night."

"No fear," I said. "Shall we bring you some fish?"

"Me pleased," he said, in English, and so we passed through.

When we were inside the naval harbour, I looked at the sea-walls near the entrance to Drake's Passage. They had done nothing there at that time to rig a boom across; nor had they any machine-gun on the wall, nor sentry-box for that matter.

"You see," I said to Tollick. "They've not barred the way yet."

"No," he said. "And now, as we fish, we'll go through this channel exactly as if we had the tow, and note every little thing. To do a job like this, you must have the whole channel like a living thing in your brain."

Very slowly, in the evening, we went down the reaches, watching the water with all our eyes. The sun was already behind the Sierras when we entered: the light slowly dimmed upon the scene, until the birds, which had been feeding upon outlying rocks, turned inland to roost. As the water dimmed, it took to gleam-

132

ing from within, as the fish moved or darted.
We had caught a great many fish, that lay
slapping in the scuppers.

Presently, as we fished in the Boneyard,
there came a shattering crash from the gun
on Nun's Point far astern. It was followed by
the cries and flights of startled birds, and distant bugle-calls. "That's the gun," Tollick
said. "They'll have closed the booms now. We
may just stay fishing."

Not long after the gunfire, but before the
darkness had set in, a motor-boat from the fort
on Drake's Islet came out towards us. Seeing
uniforms in the stern sheets, I feared that they
had come to order us out of the channel, or at
least to ask what we were. The uniformed men
turned out to be two subalterns from the gar-
rison come for an evening's fishing; seeing that
we were getting bites, they remained not far
from us, catching several good fish and sometimes holding them up for us to see. When it
began to grow darkish, and stars were showing, wisps of mist began to form upon the
water, and to strike cold. They left their fishing at this, swung round and sped away towards the fort. Presently the navigation
beacons along the coast began to burn and

flash. We heard the motor-boat's engine thud away into the dusk: presently we heard the voices on the islet's landing, and a bugle-call from within the fort. After that it was dark, with a silence all about us only broken by the noise of water on the reefs, the bell-buoys, and the spouts of the Roarers.

"What will you do now, sir?" Tollick asked.

"I was thinking I could take your dory back to the naval harbour, to see if they've barred the way in."

"No need to take a boat, sir," Tollick said, "we'll take the tug there. It will be practice for us, and save you a long row."

"Take the tug part of the way," I said, "then let me row the rest; they'll probably have patrol-boats cruising."

"Right, sir," he said, "we'll go on until we're stopped: that's always the best way."

I have seen nothing more beautiful than that space of reefs on the journey back towards the harbour. It was dark water, sown with stars, and streaking into fire wherever a fish moved or a reef broke surface. The city on its low hills to the westward made a great bank of lights, which shone in lines and half-moons, with a few soft crimson stars over the theatres.

Part of the President's festa that night was a firework display for the citizens. Some few rockets were already being loosed from time to time against the clear, still glowing sky, in which the Evening Star burned.

Tollick, Harry and I checked all our estimates for the second time. They told me that they liked the Boneyard the least of the reaches, "because of the jobble," which they felt might make them less able to handle the tow. "I'd rather stem it than run it," Tollick said; "still, we can't have everything; that's sure."

Presently we were headed quietly to the naval harbour, where the beacons on the sea-walls were beset with faint streamers or streaks of mist. Now we were going to put it to the touch; was the entrance barred or patrolled?

We were showing the regulation lights of a steamship under way at night, and moving at about half-speed. I was forward with Harry, marvelling at the beauty and silence, as the little rollers of soft flame moved from our bows to shake themselves into spangles against the uncovered rocks at the channel sides.

We could see no boom. "There's no boom there," Harry said. "They wouldn't set a boom without lighting it."

"I don't expect a boom," I said, "but there will be patrols . . . or machine-guns on the walls."

"We should see guns or sentries," he said. "Those beacons give a good light."

We drew nearer to the gateway between the beacons. I noticed the great moths beating round the globes in which they burned, and the black, big, darting bats preying on the moths. No gun had been mounted on the walls, nor was any sentry or seaman on a beat there. We could see right into the naval harbour, all dark and clear, and spangled with lights, across which, now and then, a wraith of mist drove.

"There's no patrol-boat," Harry said.

Tollick hailed us from the wheel-house as we entered the naval harbour. "It's as you thought, sir. All clear; no gun, no boom and no patrol. I'll take her right on in and anchor in that tier where the hulks are. Then you can go ashore in the boat and tell your friends that the coast's clear. Then when you're ready, about one in the morning, you come off with them and we'll try what we've agreed."

I do not know what naval harbours are like at night in peace time as a general rule: I never

136

was in one, before nor since. That one was the most peaceful place that I have seen. It was all still, starry and empty. The ships there were all old hulks built up into store-ships, and now seemingly deserted by their watchmen. There were no boats moving there. I noticed a line of red lights low down on the water where the new boom shut us from the berth we had left. "Just as well, sir," Harry said, "that we left it when we did."

I had expected a police-boat or patrol-boat to come down upon us at our first appearance within the beacons: none came. Tollick chose a berth in a tier of hulks, rounded-to and let go his anchor, not a quarter of a mile from the *Gry*, whose "riding-lights were burning brightly," I noticed.

"Here we're well-placed, sir," Tollick said, "for when we want to take your ship."

"Here's the sea-breeze," Harry said, "to clear the air and give pneumonia." I looked round at our neighbours in the tier.

"We're just a little like the fox, shut in with the hen for the night," I said.

"No police to bother us here, sir," Tollick said, "this is naval water. We shan't be bothered, you'll find."

"How are we to find you in thick fog?" I asked.

"Easy, sir, dead easy," he answered. "You can note our direction now. If it's thick fog when you and your friends come off, listen for a special fog-signal. A ship's fog-signal here is two bells each half-minute. Well, listen for a fog-bell making three bells every half-minute; that will be us."

Harry helped me down into the little pram or dory in which I was to go ashore. "From about midnight on," he said, "we'll be looking out for you. If we don't see the pram again, well: it will be no great loss."

"One minute," I said, "I'll take some fish. If I'm stopped by a sentry I can say I've been fishing."

I strung some snappers through the gills with rope yarn, and pushed off into the mist to find my friends.

I pulled away a little out of my course so as to pass the *Gry*. One of the men on her fo'c's'le was playing a zither: the others sat about him listening. There was a light at her gangway head, and a seaman on duty there. There were lights in two of her deck cabins, where her officers (I suppose) were dressing for

138

the levée. Her gig was at her gangway, un-attended.

I pulled under her stern, to make sure that she had no stern fasts. She had none. Grau was no doubt right in his surmise, that she was left there for the night. On the morrow she would be berthed at some wharf and dis-charged, if our little plan miscarried. A sea-man who was smoking on her poop looked down upon me, and passed some remark to me which I did not hear properly. I pulled on away towards the shore, feeling (as Harry had foretold) the sea-breeze beginning to freshen on my face and the pram to travel the more readily. The wisps of mist, which had been floating and trying to settle, disappeared before the breeze. Some naval launches, towing cutters full of liberty men, came past me, going or coming to one or other of the landings. Presently I was at one of the stairs myself. I hitched the pram's painter to a bolt, and hopped on to the stairs with my fish. The stairs were crowded with naval ratings. I thrust through them to the top, hoping to be able to pass the turnstile unchallenged, but the sentry stopped me and the guardias came up.

"You a naval man?"

139

"No," I said.

"How you come?"

"I was fishing," I said, holding up my fish. "When I came back the boom was across the entrance; I had to come here."

"You English?"

"Yes."

"You no business in the naval harbour. You see the Teniente."

"Certainly," I said.

However, they were busy with their own business of searching returning liberty men for rum, and seeing the various naval guards away to the palace for the levée. I waited and waited, but was not brought before the Teniente: I was ignored. At last, catching the eye of one guardia, I showed him the edge of a ten-peseta note and winked. He came up at that; I asked him if he would care for some fish and let me see the Teniente. He said: "Sure, Mike," being a travelled man, and in a few minutes the Teniente came out smiling and let me go through. I left them the pram, the note, the fish and my blessing: it was now just after half-past nine. A taxi took me to Duke of Rivas Street, where I found Señora Grau, her husband and Tom, all three on tenterhooks, wondering what on earth had happened.

"All's well, so far," I said. "The naval harbour has been shut, but the tug is inside it, close to the *Gry*, and the Drake's Channel has neither guard nor bar."

They sighed, for relief; then, as happens to the anxious, our minds turned to other possible causes of trouble. Tom began by saying: "Suppose the *Gry's* steering gear has been dismantled, as a precaution."

I ended that by saying: "It had not been a few hours ago when they shifted her berth."

Tom then said: "Suppose her compass is untrustworthy." Grau and I at once said that she need not steer a compass course, but follow the tug, and conform to what the tug did. Then we debated points about the steering: would she be an unhandy cow to steer: would the wind get up and put a lop in the channel with sets of current this way or that: would there be variable currents or jobbles coming at odd times of the tide across any of the way? Other thoughts cropped up and were mentioned:

Suppose the fog sets in too thick?

Suppose the tug men betray us?

Suppose somebody else betrays us?

Suppose we try to get the *Gry* but are arrested or knocked on the head?

Suppose we get her and run her ashore?

Suppose we get her and are pursued and caught?

Don't think that we were scared. We were resolute to make the attempt; that was beyond question. We were only anxious to be doing and found that the waiting made us nervous.

"Now, come," Señora Grau said, "this will not do. Here it is, only ten o'clock: we are all as nervous as we can be, with a couple of hours still to wait. Suppose we all go to a cinema to take our minds off it, till nearer the time." This was the wisest supposing that we had supposed: we went out.

It is a good many years since we went to that cinema: and I have forgotten the name of it, it was about a Southern Republic, whose President robbed the Treasury, and escaped to live happily ever afterwards in the south of Spain. It put new heart into us. We all took it as a good omen, that the image of a successful fraud should appear to us at that time. In the midst of it, reaches of Drake's Passage floated into my mind like pictures, of reef and rock with the water white upon them, and the two

Roarers spouting and giving tongue, the bell-buoys clanging and the Boneyard waiting.

Probably, during the war, every man had some horrible hours of waiting for something to begin, that would be grim enough in the being, and yet was grimmer in the waiting for. That night in the cinema was a sort of fore-taste of the war to me. Presently it would be time to start, and then there would be dangers, like the leaps at Aintree, the police, the naval patrols, the possible treacheries: the probable accidents and the fog that was almost certain. Now and then, when lights went up after the reels, I could see Señora Grau impassive, Grau with his lower jaw working oddly as he swallowed, Tom rather white and strained, thinking, as he told me afterwards, of moments in the fighting at Santa Ana, when things had seemed to be going wrong. Presently the performance ended: we were quit of shelter and warmth and light: we were for outlawry and what chance might bring.

When we were back at Duke of Rivas Street, we helped Señora Grau to prepare a meal: sardines, a darkish bread, rather sweet to taste, some raisins of the sun and oranges. She made us coffee in a big blue and white jug. We drank

143

big bowls of it made syrupy with sugar candy: after this we smoked yellow Santa Barbara cigarettes.

Presently, Señora Grau opened one of the windows, and let in a fresh draught of air from the sea-breeze that was now dying, and with it, of course, the noise of the surf on the outer breakwater.

"It is a wonderful noise, the surf," she said.

"The sea-breeze always touches up the surf," Grau said, "but it is dying down now."

We listened to it for a moment. Apart from the noise of the clicking curtain-rings and the roll of the water breaking there was almost no noise in that quiet alley: perhaps the clop of a horse going by with a calèche, or the bell of a religious house. Then, in the midst of the silence, we heard rather far away the notes of a band playing: "We will rally round the banner of our fathers." "Ca y est," Grau said, "the band is playing the opening of the gates for the reception."

"Time to dress," Tom said.

We went into another room, where Tom's new uniform was laid out. Some serges were there for me, but I thought it wiser to come as I was, as a member of the tug's English crew.

Grau dressed elsewhere in a staff-lieutenant's uniform.

When we met again in the salon, Señora Grau joined us. She wore the black mantilla of her race, but I believe she thought that she was dressed as Mrs. Tollick.

We all shook hands; Señora Grau poured out for each of us a little golden liqueur which she called the Kiss of Peace. We drank to each other and wished our adventure good luck. I am sure that the three good Catholics prayed. I just hoped that somehow I might help Tom to pull it off. Then we went down the stairs and out of doors. The door closed behind us, shutting us out from safety among outlaws and defiers of the peace.

We turned towards the Front, noting that the sea-wind had now died. People do not seem to go to bed in Santa Barbara: the streets were often populous till two in the morning. However, on that night, the crowds had gone to the palace to see the sights of the levée and to hear the band: the streets down to the water-front were quiet, save for two men strolling slowly down, one of them playing a mandoline, the other humming.

Tom and Grau walked in front, Señora

145

Grau and I followed. Señora Grau carried a little dispatch-case: I had a hand-bag containing a lead-line, with a seven-pound lead, and a Thompson's Indicator; I kept saying to myself, "After use at sea this instrument must be soaked for an hour in fresh water before being oiled and put away."

We came out upon the silent, still water-front where no breath of breeze now blew. We saw the lights on the water, and the flash of the occulting beacons.

"There's the fog," Tom said. He nodded towards a streak like a ghostly shore lying across the reef a mile away.

"It is settling in," Grau said, after he had watched it for an instant.

"Come on. Right turn," Tom said. We turned to the right and walked on, as before.

As we crossed the public gardens in the glare of the arc-lights, some naval ratings, who were lounging on the benches there, leaped to attention and saluted. Tom returned the salute gravely. We walked on with our hearts beating and our minds empty, but all focused on a point of excitement.

"There's the prize," Tom said, pausing to look to seaward. "Where's your *Slasher?*"

146

"Beyond her, a little to the left," I said; "the mist is on her now."

"You'd better say 'My Captain' when you speak to me," Tom said.

"Yes, my Captain."

"Good. Come on, then. There's the naval landing pier ahead. We are for it now."

The naval landing pier looked outwardly like a suburban railway station. It was a sort of shed, with many printed regulations hung on its outer walls. Inside the door were turnstiles with sentry-boxes. The sentry, who had been having a quiet cigarette, dashed up to the turnstile as we approached, and unhooked the catch of the turnstile before he saluted. "Moon and Star," Tom said, returning the salute; and so we passed in without any question.

In the covered space beyond the turnstile there were two small naval guns mounted on field-gun carriages (for seamen practising "landing-party" probably). I remember that there were some leather fire-buckets in a rack: they were painted red, and contained a lot of cigarette-ends. At the sides of the jetty head one heard the lap and slop of water, touched up against the piles by some boat passing in the harbour. I could see bright lights on the water

147

from the moored torpedo-boats close in.

"Sentry," Tom said, "what men have you here in the guard-room?"

"Six, my Captain," the man replied.

"I want them," Tom said. "Fall them out."

The sentry saluted, went to the guard-room, and "fell them out." They were a sort of squad for the master-at-arms. They were there, as I suppose, to search returning leave men for spirits. They were in the naval undress of vests and working-trousers. They lined up and stood to attention.

"I want two more," Tom said. "Sentry, go call those two men from the street there."

"The sentry's not supposed to stir, sir," the sentry stammered. "Not from his post."

"Go call them," Tom said, and the man did. The two men came in, wondering, from the street. They were both first-class seamen dressed for an evening's leave: they were plainly much puzzled at being called, but seeing an officer in a blaze of gold lace, they saluted.

"I want you," Tom said. "Fall in here." So they fell in.

"Sentry," Tom said, "call me a steam picket-boat."

"Is it the Admiral's launch, sir?" the sentry asked.

"Yes," Tom said.

"Will you wait for just one moment, sir," the sentry said, "there is a party coming . . ."

"Let the party through, you," Tom said to one of the seamen. "And you, sentry, call me the launch."

The sentry ran to the jetty side and blew two shrill blasts on his whistle, which were answered at once by a picket-boat lying at a little distance from the pier. At the same time a small party of naval ratings, in charge of a petty officer, came to the turnstile, gave the pass-word, and came through to where we stood. They were defaulters, I think, who had been doing fatigue of some sort in the President's palace, washing dishes very likely. They stared at Tom's uniform, pretty hard, as they stood at attention. They belonged to the prison-ship *Retribucion*; their boat and guard were waiting for them. The sentry returned to Tom, saluted, and said:

"The Admiral's steam launch is alongside, sir."

Tom turned to his eight men, told them to right turn and get into the launch. They right-turned and went. Tom and we three others followed, to where a fine big steam launch lay alongside the jetty, with the bowfast and stern-fast men both ashore, standing at attention, with their caps off. We could see the engine men in the glow of the well, also standing at attention. Tom hopped down into the stern sheets and took his seat under the coloured awning: Grau followed him: I helped Señora Grau aboard: together we made ourselves small well forward from Tom and Grau. The naval ratings ignored us, I suppose, as civilians of some sort, beneath their notice.

"Sentry," Tom called.

"Sir."

"Have you blankets in the guard-room?"

"Yes, sir."

"Bring them for these men then."

The sentry brought the blankets. Tom told the eight men who were clustered forward to wrap themselves against the cold, for the night struck chill, with the fog coming. They did as they were bid.

"Let go aft," Tom said. "Shove ahead, engineer." Without any question, the men obeyed.

"Let go forward," Tom said, "shove off."

So far there had been not the least hitch anywhere: the way had been made smooth for us
beyond our dreams. Here there came a little
hitch. The bowman, though a smart hand,
slipped as he cast loose forward and fell rather
clumsily among the men in the boat's bows. It
was not a pleasant omen to myself, I must say.

"Are you hurt there, bowman?" Tom asked.

"No, sir, thank you, sir."

The boat was one of great power, the engineer sheered her off at speed. "Where for, sir?"
he asked.

"On service out towards the reef," Tom said.
"We've to board a tug there. Go slow till we
see her."

"Ay, ay, sir."

We were silent enough on that passage.

I kept track of our course as we drove out
towards the reef; now and then I passed the
word to Grau, who told the coxswain. The
men forward from me huddled into their
blankets, not speaking, though they must have
wondered what kind of service they were
pressed for. Before we had gone three hundred
yards the wisps of fog were curling about us.
"Go slow," Tom said to the coxswain. "Slower
yet: we may miss her in this fog."

Presently, we were past the *Gry*. There was the *Slasher* on our port bow, with the smoke rising white from her funnel. I pointed her out to Grau, who told the coxswain to bring her alongside the tug there. This he did smartly, with a word to the launchees to tend their boat-hooks. A tug-hand dropped down a line: then Harry rowsed over the side a rope-ladder with wooden treads, by which Tom and I went aboard the tug. Leaning down over the side, Harry and I helped Señora Grau on board. Tom told Grau to stay in the launch, drop astern on the line, and wait for a few minutes.

"Where's Captain Tollick?" Tom asked.

"I'm sorry to say," the Mate said, "I'm sorry indeed to have to say, that he's had cruel news by the mail, and his heart is broken!"

"Do you mean that he is dead?"

"No, sir," Harry said, "not dead; but it's laid him low. It's about his son."

"Can I see him?" Tom asked.

"Yes, sure, sir," Harry said. "But I don't think he'll answer you. I've known Joe Cæsar like it before, over his son. He's all heart, Joe, though you might never think it, to look at him. Come along to his cabin, sir."

Julius Cæsar Tollick was sitting on the hard

black horse-hair top of his locker. He looked as though the spine and every nervous power in him had been suddenly removed. The change from a few hours before, when he had been so alert, lively and quick, ready to take in every point and to act upon it, was shocking. His face was gone grey and ghastly. The moustache and whiskers had a collapsed look. He didn't seem to see us. His eyes were fixed on some picture of misery which we could neither see nor share.

"Joe, old man," Harry said, "here's the Captain come to see you."

Tollick shook his head a little, but paid no attention.

"Won't you speak to him, Joe?" Harry said. "You'd be better if you could shake it off a little and take your mind off it."

Tollick did not show that he had heard.

"Joe," Harry said again. "You'll rouse and bitt, won't you? It's time for us to be getting to it, getting under way with these gentlemen."

We waited for a full minute for some sign of thought or deed from the broken man: none came. "It's no good," Harry said, "it has hit him too hard, this time. We'd better leave him."

When we were out on deck again, Tom asked Harry if he would take charge in place of Tollick; and attempt the channel without him.

"I'll try, of course, sir," Harry said. "The tug's ready. But without Joe I'm only half a man. We've worked together for years and we work as one."

"You do, indeed," I said. "I suppose Captain Tollick would have steered, while you would have been forward? I've got the hang of the channel, and something of the way you work. Let me be forward, while you steer. I won't let you down."

"I'm sure you won't, sir," Harry said.

"I've got the channel in my head," I said.

"Yes, sir," Harry said, "you're a pilot, but this is more a question of towage; reckoning what to allow for this and that. However, no man can make a better pudding than what he's got groceries for."

It was not complimentary, but there was sense in it.

"You'll do it together," Tom said. "You'd do it alone."

"I shall miss Joe," Harry said.

"I won't get in the way," I said.

"But may I suggest something? We've got a steam launch here, why not let the steam launch go down the channel ahead of us?"

"No, no, sir," Harry said. "We might use a boat ahead in a dock, when going through a dock-gate in a fog, but not in a job like this. We'll be all right, sir."

"What about a Distance Indicator on the rail here?" I asked.

"No, no, sir. We're not used to it. Use is second nature. You'd better leave me to my own way."

"We'll need a leadsman in the first two reaches," I said.

"There's Alf here," he said, indicating a shock-headed lad. "We've kept Alf sober for you. He's a fair young tank when there's vino going: aren't you, Alf?"

Alf grinned, but did not speak.

"Have you a stage and breast-rope rigged?"

"All ready, sir."

"Very well, then," Tom said, "we'll get to it, if you please. I'll go aboard and take the *Gry*. You trip your anchor and come down to us."

He blew a whistle to Grau, hailed the launch and ordered her to haul up alongside.

When they had drawn in, he ordered Grau

and two of the seamen to come aboard the tug. "You will be in charge here," he said to Grau, "until she is safely alongside the tow. You, Charles, will stay on board and arrange with the Mate."

"Very good, my Captain," we said, saluting.

He was just about to go down into the launch, when he turned to me, and said, "If we fail, then beat it, muy pronto, in the tug to the rendezvous written here." He handed me a leaf from a bridge-order book. "Very good, my Captain," I said, saluting again. "And good luck, sir."

"Thanks," he said, poising himself upon the rail. Seeing his chance, he dropped down into the launch and bade her shove off.

There was much mist floating about us at that instant. Wreathing as it did about the men in the launch it gave me an odd picture of heads detached from bodies. All in the boat looked like souls ridded of their flesh. They sheered away from us into the mist. At the same instant our cable began to rattle in.

Of course, I saw that Grau had to stay in the tug, to give a naval air to her when she reached the *Gry,* but I found it hard to let Tom go aboard the *Gry* alone, to play the game single-handed: however, it had to be. I was near Harry for a moment as the anchor came home.

"Fog's coming in quickly," I said.

"Ah, it won't be much, sir," he said, "nothing but a little mist. Why, I'd breathe a better fog than you'd get here." He moved away into the wheel-house to take the wheel. A stout, elderly tug-hand, with a smiling face, sang out to him how the cable grew: in a couple of minutes we were under way, swinging round slowly towards the *Gry*, through wafts of vapour which drifted in streaks against our masthead light and disappeared. Often wafts of mist seemed thick ahead, until we reached them, but as we touched them they died. Somebody aft, lighting the hawsers clear, was singing:

"The girls so wile me
And so beguile me
I don't know what to say,
So as quickly as a comet
I shall follow old Mahomet
And have a different wife for every day."

In five minutes we had passed under the stern of the *Gry* and were coming up on her starboard side, where the launch was now lying, at her ladder-foot.

The launchees were still in their boat. Tom's pressed men were somewhere aboard the *Gry*. What had happened? I wondered. What luck had Tom's bluff had?

Evidently good luck, so far, because Tom himself hailed us from the *Gry's* forward well, as we sidled slowly in. He called to Grau in Spanish to see the tug's hawsers bent to the lines he was throwing, and then to transfer himself and the naval ratings on board the *Gry*. Grau answered, saluting; the *Gry's* lines were flung down and caught: then Grau and the two seamen scrambled up the side and got aboard her. (Señora Grau remained in the tug.)

I saw the seamen in the *Gry* (there were about a dozen of them with our recruits) dipping our hawsers clear and passing them forward, while we slowly went ahead of her to take position to tow. It is not a long job for a dozen trained, smart seamen, well-led, to get towing lines secured, but it seemed to me to take a long time.

"They'll have to slip that cable of theirs," I said to myself, "for they've no steam to get it by."

As far as I could make out, they secured our hawsers forward, and then passed somewhere out of hearing. I had gone into the tug's eyes, which was to be my station, expecting that we should start as soon as the lines were fast. However, the *Gry's* cable was not slipped and no signal came to us to shove ahead. I waited and waited, expecting the hail at each instant. What on earth was keeping them? Why didn't they slip and let us go? At any instant, the police or a patrol might come down upon us.

At last, I could stand it no more, but laid aft, to try to find out what was the matter.

We were lying by waiting for the signal. Some of the tug hands had come aft to learn the cause of the delay. We leaned together, staring through the mist at the *Gry*. She loomed out at us there, under her towing lights. I could make out a figure, probably Grau, on her forecastle, but did not hail, for we wanted as little shouting as possible.

"What's keeping them?" I asked.

One of the tug-hands said, "I suppose the cable-shackles." Another said, "They might be buoying the slip, sir."

I thought it much more likely that the crew

had become suspicious about what was being done. They might be aft somewhere Morsing the shore, or putting Tom through the Third Degree. Yet that unconcerned figure on the forecastle must be Grau.

I found Señora Grau beside me. She had been the calmest of us all that evening; she was the calmest still.

"It is hard to have to wait, like this," I said.

"Ah," she answered, "I knew that there would be a wait, for the crew has to pack before going ashore."

"Why, of course," I said, "why didn't I think of that? Of course, all hands are below now, packing their bags."

That was the cause of the delay: she was right; but I did not know it till later: and at the moment it gave no comfort, for the thought at once followed: "If they are below together, packing their bags, they will talk, and one or other of them is certain to suspect something and tell the others." The only comfort was, that in the gathering mist they could hardly Morse to the shore or to the neighbouring ships.

I tried not to show my anxiety, but the strain of waiting there, when the lines had been secured and the way to sea was clear, was very great.

Close to me in that little tug was a warm, lit doorway from which came the noise of engines and the smell of oil and hot metal. Two of the engine-room staff, I know not their rank, were leaning there, getting a cool breath in the interval of waiting. They talked together about various subjects. One of them said that what he was suffering from the last time he was in England was "a little catarrh." The other said that he had never had catarrh, but he'd heard tell of it, and did it make you swell? They talked, then, of diseases which did make you swell, or even burst; and then as there were not many of these, they began to talk of the job in hand.

The catarrh man said: "This stealing a ship's piracy, ain't it, mate?"

The other replied: "Not when a navy does it; then it's glory."

Then the first said: "I suppose it's the stone jug if they get us?"

"That's the ticket," the other answered. "Me I O U if you win and me heartfelt sympathy if you come a mucker."

"Right ho," said the first, "so Alleluia,

brothers; step up front."

The delay became less and less endurable. That part of the harbour was deserted, and nobody, seemingly, had heard us or suspected us. The way out to sea was still fairly clear. Why could we not snatch the heaven-sent instant and be gone. We could not count on much more clearness, because while I stood there biting my fingers, the big foghorn at the lighthouse on Nun's Point began to blare, which meant that real fog was beginning. A minute or two later the tinkle of the fog-bells began from the ships in the tiers. The irregular, silvery ting-ting of two bells came from perhaps fifty ships. A big ship out at sea blew her siren and some lesser ship replied.

Near us, as it happened, it was not yet very thick. I went aft again, meaning to hail the *Gry* and have my doubts resolved.

I could no longer see the figure waiting on the fo'c's'le there, nor even the *Gry*, save as a sort of bulk looming out; but Grau hailed at that instant.

"Ahoy, the tug there."

"Sir."

"I'm ready to slip. Will you shove ahead and hold her?"

"Ay, ay, sir. Is your launch clear?"

"The launch is just shoving off now."

"Let her get clear, sir," I shouted, "and then trip your ladder."

I heard the launch thresh water as she sheered away from the *Gry* with all the naval ratings. I heard the creak of the tackle as Tom and Grau together tripped the ladder. Then with a rattle and roar followed by a shock and a splash, the *Gry's* cable leapt over the bitts, through the hawse pipes to the sea.

"Full ahead," Grau shouted.

We had been moving very slightly forward for thirty seconds: now with a noise of snapping and snibbing the hawsers tautened, squeezing the drops out. Our screw threshed, seemed to take hold and then to drive us. The trembling in the *Slasher* changed to the regular beat of an advance: we were off.

I went forward to stare into the mist ahead. When we had plucked the *Gry* from her berth we drew her clear of the outer tier and straightened her out for the entrance to Drake's Channel. The fog was growing upon us slowly, in waves and wafts followed by intervals of clearness. The beacons on the sea-wall dead ahead were sometimes fuzzes of yellow, sometimes invisible.

So often, when a ship gets under way, the police-boats dart down upon her: they are like flies that attack the animal that moves from shelter. I felt certain that our movement would cause their movement and bring them about us. It did not.

What struck me most at that instant was the beauty of the singing of a liberty party in some boat not now visible near the landing stairs. They had a couple of flutes with them playing the Evening Hymn to which the men sang. The flute music came like a blessing to us: it made the hymn one of the most lovely things I have heard.

Slowly we drew nearer to the beacons, and entered plumb between them, into Drake's Channel, where one could see nothing but swathe after white swathe rolling down upon the lights we cast. The fog closed in astern of us and shut us away from fear of police and patrol-boats, for that time. I counted the revolutions, and reckoned our advance, while I listened for our only guide, the East Roarer.

"There's always a bit of luck in these things," Harry had said. We had had a bit of luck in getting into the channel right dead between the marks. Would the luck hold at the bend, and at the next bend and the bend beyond?

You may have watched a ship's company in a tense situation, and noticed how silent and intent they will be. I was there, "in the eyes" on the port bow, staring forward; alongside me, on the starboard bow, was the man called Hawky, also staring forward. Behind me, ready with his lead, on the stage, was Alf. Further aft, in the lighted wheel-box, was Harry, steering. What if his steering lights gave out?

I knew that the lead would help me in one part of that reach, about 500 yards from the entrance. I waited for that, reckoning our distance run, 300 yards, two cables, 450 yards. "Cast here," I said to Alf.

Just at that point, right in the centre of the channel, there is a patch of white sand, with shells and small, broken coral on it, at a depth of just over five fathoms. It is in the midst of the narrowest part of the Wrist, and measures about fifty yards long by thirty broad. Alf cast his lead, called "A half five," hauled-in, looked at the arming, reported, "Shell and that," brushed away the scraps from the grease, cast again, called "Quarter less six. Shell and that," and hauled-in for a third cast. But at the third cast we were over the patch of sand; he brought up a dinted arming at quarter six. I judged that we were six hundred yards on our way to the East Roarer, with a cable still to go before that first right-angled turn.

The East Roarer cried out aloud ahead within a cable from us: "150 yards," I reckoned, in that subtraction sum always going on in my head. I had arranged with Harry that I was to leave the changing of course to him: he would do all that by his own methods and mother wit, but that I was to yell "like fun," if I sighted any boat fishing or any ship at anchor; or if I found the tug suddenly on the top of any of her marks. I ticked off the yards in my head, revolution by revolution, till the suspense was almost unbearable: then, suddenly, far away, behind me, as it seemed, on my starboard quarter, I heard a distant bell-buoy give a melancholy clang. I knew that it was the bell-buoy on the Widow's Crook, and marvelled how it could be on my quarter. My heart stood still at the sound from fear that we had held on too far. Then I realised that it was on its right bearing, or was it right? "No," I thought, "it isn't right: we're fifty yards too far to the east."

Then in the darkness of the fog ahead, quite close to us as it seemed, the East Roarer uttered his bellow, with a spatter and splash of collapsing water following the roar. There was no gleam to be seen: the fog was thick now, but I judged that it was the instant, and Harry judged so, too: the wheel chains rattled. Shouts passed aft to the *Gry* till Grau repeated them. The tug heeled a little to starboard, and trembled and checked as she came round. The hawsers grided as they swung: there was a sort of hesitation in our movement as though the *Gry* were not sure that she would not take a sheer and pile herself up, but she came round, and steadied to the new course, with the East Roarer gurgling astern, and both bell-buoys distinctly audible almost on the same bearing.

"That's her first fence," I said to Hawky. "She's over that: now for the next."

We crept on as before, with my heart in my boots, for this second reach was made narrow by the sandbank and somehow I felt that Harry had held on too long, and had not allowed for the sand. We had been plumb on our course for entering the first reach: how right we were for this one I could not tell, but my instinct told me that we were not right. It was a matter for our Fortune, and the skill of Harry. In a narrow sleeve like that, with rock on both sides and a shelf of sand in the middle, a very tiny error in the course will pile you up.

All our time in that middle reach it was as thick as fog could be. I could not see Hawky beside me nor even a blur of light in the wheel-house. We were crawling into a blind darkness, with no guide save the bell-buoys, one of which was now drawing near. "Get a cast now," I said to Alf. He got a couple of casts, with fair depth, and with sand on the arming, which showed that we were near the danger. "We're too much to port," I said to myself. "We're too far over to port. Harry's hung on to her too long." I was holding my breath, and biting my nails: and then, just at the instant that I feared, there came from astern the feeling of a dead-weight suddenly applied, checking our way, and that sensation, half-sound, half-sense, of squeezing and sticking. The *Gry* was on the sandbank, and holding us.

There was no noise at all. Harry rang his telegraph for full speed ahead: our engines

doubled and the screws threshed. After an instant's pause, the *Gry* shifted forward, and
slithered off it after us, checking again for an
instant, then moving on. We were past it.

"We were nearly stuck there," I said to
Hawky. "I knew we were too far to port."

"She's over it, sir," Hawky said.

That was the danger which I had feared
most: we had hit it a glancing blow, and had
scraped past it, luckily, instead of sticking.
The scare of the blow took away what little
peace of mind I had left. I began to think:
"That isn't what Tollick and Harry reckoned
as the danger. The real danger to them was
that running jobble in the Boneyard; and what
they count dangerous is probably deadly." I
began to see now why a jobble would be dangerous.

In that blindness of the middle reach and the
stillness of the fog, there was always, at every
point, the wash and splash of water crawling
and slipping over reefs. Presently I began to
hear the voice of a more turbulent water, which
grew much louder as we neared it. I knew that
this voice was the jobble. I knew from its tone
of voice that it was running much harder than
it had run in the afternoon: and the threat of

its leaping gaggle told me that it would take us and the tow where it chose, and that we should have no say in the matter. However, Harry knew all that better than I did. Anyhow, there would be no fishers fishing there, nor any ship anchored. I might as well leave my post.

The water of this race was soon roaring athwart our hawse just ahead. The bell-buoy, which had been on our bow, now drew away to our beam. Then our bows lifted and bowed down with a plowter.

The quiet path of the *Slasher* suddenly changed to a dance upon a mill-race which shook her to her bearings. As she lifted and splashed well into it, Harry "let her have it." We came round like a weather-cock. There followed a sickening instant, no, half a minute, while the *Gry* felt the change, tried not to conform to it, and then found the jobble too much for her, and swung round after us. She was round. But in the dance of that current who could tell where we should finish: the ship was no longer in control.

"Sir," Hawky said, "will you look at that? Did you ever see the beat of that?"

"That," was a lifting of all fog from the

path before us, and the display of the third reach straining dark in the jobble, but in all other parts lighted by phosphorescence. Wherever the water was still each rock burned in a glow as though myriads of glow-worms were at pasture on them. On the sides of the channel the effect was something like lighted rime-frost. Something luminous was in the spout of the West Roarer as it shot aloft dead ahead, giving us our course. "There's sinner's luck," I said, "just at the instant we needed it most."

I remembered that in the earlier flood that afternoon the jobble had ceased to be a race about midway down the Boneyard. I prayed that that might be so at that state of the tide, for if not we should smash. We went down that reach in double-quick time under the shove of the current; and I suppose at each second of the run we risked losing our tow, for we had no real hold of her. She seemed inclined to take charge and get across the stream: she very nearly did: but just didn't until the end of the rush, when the jobble checked against the in-coming flood, and gave us a chance to straighten her. We regained control, and made that last turn round a bend in a clear moment when we got good bearings of the lights that would guide us to open water. Never was such luck.

The danger now was that a patrol would come to us from the Naval Station on Drake's Island; but our luck held: the fog came down in earnest, shutting out everything, even the hand held at an arm's length from the eyes. We went full speed ahead till we knew, what the tug's movements told us, that we were at sea, then we altered course for the rendezvous arranged. Presently, even the noise of the great hooter on Nun's Point could no longer be heard: we were far out at sea.

Just before the dawn, when there was colour in the sky, and light to see, the fog thinned away, with promise of a clear morning. Julius Cæsar Tollick came out from his cabin to us; he walked like a body without a soul: I have never seen a man so broken.

Harry handed over the wheel to Hawky, so that he might speak to his Captain.

"How is it, Joe?" he asked.

"I let you in for all the trouble last night," Tollick answered, "but I see you brought her out."

"Ah, it was nothing," Harry said, "the fog

was nothing, and the channel isn't like some. There's good deep water on it."

"I've been thinking," Tollick said, "that a man with rum in his veins ought never to have children. My father, who was a boatswain's mate in Admiral Hornby's Flying Squad, was a drinker, never sober ashore. And I'm a drinker, too. If you would look at a bottle of rum or brandy you would think it was coloured water, for it must have been rain water once. But it isn't water. It's a poison that runs in men and in their children.

"What is the thing children ought to have beyond all others? Not food, or clothes or shelter or school, but good clean parents who've got no poison in them.

"My father had the poison of rum in him, and so have I, and so has my son, the Rooter, who went into the motor-cars; and now they've locked up my son for dangerous driving when drunk. Yet it is me they should have locked up: me and my father before me."

He moved away to the side and stared at the sunrise.

"He feels it, Joe," Harry said, " his son, that he's so proud of, the Rooter as he calls him, he's a hurtler when he draws his pay: a fair young rip."

Tollick came back to us. "I see what it is," he said, "very few people have the right to have children, and those who take the right ought to suffer. My married life began in rum. If I'd not had that other rum-hot I would never have asked my Jane; and all this wouldn't have been."

"Joe, Joe," Harry said soothingly, "she would have caught you without the rum-hot. Feelings get hot without any rum to help them; and no man dodges his fate."

"No, no," Tollick said, "it's like casting from moulds. Children ought only to be cast from good moulds: and I'm a bad mould, that ought to be in the dust-bin. Still," he said, rousing, "we'll drop down to the tow now. This young gentleman and lady would like to get aboard her to their friends, and we'll drop the river hawser and give her a long sea-line."

He brought the tug alongside, so that Señora Grau and I could scramble up the ladder to her.

I relieved Tom at the wheel, while the tug went ahead again, giving us a full scope. Presently the sun came over the horizon and the thinning mist grew thinner. The Graus went below to forage for breakfast for us. We were well clear of the land, of course: it lay in mist astern, with the peaks above it like faint pink clouds. My thought was that by this time the Santa Barbara destroyers would be quartering the sea for us, and that as the mist thinned we should be sighted.

"Tom," I said, "tell me how you managed last night. What happened, when you came aboard?"

Tom was shaken and tired and white, but he grinned at the question. "They leaped out of their skins at the sight of all this gold lace," he said. "The lieutenant was ashore with his gig's crew and the leading-seaman-in-charge was drunk. I gave him a piece of my mind about it. Then I told him to trim the binnacle lamps, hoist the towing lights, get the hawsers aboard, and have all clear forward for slipping. He was so afraid of being disrated that he turned to and made the others turn to. They were a very smart lot. I thought that they might suspect when I sent them to pack their bags, but no: they went away in the launch like lambs. Your plan worked like a charm, Charles, from the very first."

The two Graus appeared with a tray of hot

coffee, brown bread, honey and passion-fruit.
Señora Grau, always tidy, was now smart:
Grau looked as though he had been in the
chain-locker: his staff-officer's uniform was
ruined. We were still at breakfast there on the
bridge when Tom suddenly said: "There's the
flotilla," pointing to four little smudges ahead.

In a few minutes these neared us. They were
the escort of destroyers from El Puño, sent
to bring us in.

They brought us to El Puño, and there they
shipped me back to Santa Barbara by a night-
flying aeroplane over the frontier and a fast
car into the city. I was back in the Club fifty-
four hours after leaving Duke of Rivas Street.
No one suspected my share in the lifting of the
Gry. I asked no questions about her, but by
listening I found out, in time, that she had not
been missed for fifteen hours after we had
started.

Our naval details had gone to barracks as
ordered. The lieutenant who had gone to the
levée, slept at his club and did not attempt to
return on board until the afternoon. On looking for his ship, one of his crew told him that
she had been taken over by a superior officer
during the night. He would have been content

with this answer, had not all his clothes been in the *Gry,* and in his efforts to find the ship he roused suspicions in some breasts that all was not well. However, by this time, the Admiralty Harbour Officer had gone home into the country, and his office was closed until the morning. Just as we drew into a wharf at El Puño, the Santa Barbara Admiralty learned that the *Gry* had disappeared. It was then too late in the day to do much, except fuss and be furious.

The Poiret guns on board the *Gry* ended the war in Santa Ana by breaking the President's army at the Salt Pans outside the city. The President resigned and fled the country: Tom's party triumphed. The *Slasher* and her crew are at El Puño still, as parts of the Santano Navy. However, that is outside my story: I only wished to tell you about the taking of the *Gry.*

APPENDIX

I HAVE been asked to name the authorities for Drake's voyage to the two sea-ports. The only one known to me is Nathaniell Clutterbucke's "True Relation of Sir Frauncis Drake's late fortunat voiage to the Indies wherein he captured the carack called the *Golden Fount* at the Spaniards' city of Santanoes, and did hold to his mercy their rich capital of Santa Barbaro (more barbarous than Saint) with other spoils of their pride no less fortunat than valiant, together with some account of a new discovered iland named after the Queen's Majestie by Nathaniell Clutterbucke a master gunner in Sir Frauncis owne ship who was present at those Tragedies (to our Enemies, tho to us mirthfull Comedies) and now writes the same to show how farr English Simplicitie outgoes the Spanyard's Arrogance and to answer the Lyes of Don Francesco de Menendes their Captaine (soe-called) etc., etc."

At Santa Ana, Drake sailed boldly in in two pinnaces right under the guns of the castle, and boarded, cut out and escaped with two of the ships of the Silver Fleet. The ships were mauled in going out by the fort's guns, but Drake got them both to sea, pillaged them and cast them adrift. One of them, the *Golden Fount,* was good prize, "having in her 350 barres of silver, and much curious gold-worke, wh our Admirall did make soe bolde as to pouch up in revenge of those late Indignities practised on him at St. John Dullow." In the other, "though the Spaniards had made their treasure coy, as it were some shy Virgin, yett did our Mariners not scruple to proceede beyond the bounds of Modestie, and did find good store of bezoar stones and gum benjamine . . ."

At Santa Barbara, which Drake visited later, with his fleet, the Spaniards blocked the harbour-entrance against him, "wh hee perceiving thought to practise some subtletie where they leaste expected, therefore re-moving thence some miles he founde a present anchorage noe lesse commodious than safe in ten fathom water near a small iland lying to the south and east in wh gusheth a faire springe of pleasant cleare running water. Here hee did secure his ships against anie practice that our enemies might endeavour, and refreshed his wearie crews with sallet grass from the iland and the fishe whereof

179

was marvellous plentie, so muche that had wee had salte as wee had will we had there found our account. Yett in this plentie did not our Admirall relent his purpose of present war, but sought in his daintie pinnasses, a way into the haven, through the reefes and rockes wh make as it were a verie helle for him that would adventure.

"And as the stone yieldeth to the dropping of water, and the wood giveth to the licking of the fire, and the barred door to the importunacie of him that would enter, soe did that maze or Troya of rockes and shelfes show forth to his constant sounders a verie waie or channel, by the wh, his stoute hearte helping, hee did presentlie convey his fleet within the haven withoute the losse of anie the least plancke.

"The Spaniardes, as seeing their door in a maner forced were sore astonied, for they had not judged that anie living, above the qualitie of an herring, might have used that channel. Whereupon, seeing their astonishment, and being loath to give his enemie occasion to rallie, our Admirall, like Cæsar in his fortunat camp, hung out his bloodie flag, and waved them amaine, whereto they on their side, in a maner brag, discharged from their platforme a jollie hot volley of shott, whereof one strake the *Tyger* and hurt Mr. Edward Glubbe into the side. Yett wee, disdaining present death, maugre their ordnance, valiantlie pressed in, and presentlie drave them beyond the citie, wh then rendered to mercie.

"Wee had here a marvellous spoile of silver, so as no man perhaps hath seene the like, with good store likewise of daintie ruske and cassavi (their maner bread) with dried meates and fishe, likewise of wine in abundance, the wh awaited there the coming of the K of Spaines' fleet, with all of which wee as conquerors did make bold, notwithstanding they shot daily at us yet did not dare to come to push of pike: in the wh skirmishing we took the nephew of the Governor of Tolou, who gave for his ransom three great quoits of gold. Their Governor, fearing lest wee being disappointed of our market might fire the citie, compounded for the ransom thereof in six thousand duckets of gold, the wh hee verie honestlie paid, and wee when we had refreshed ourselves and laden our ships with what we needed, pleasantlie received, and so sailed on the 19th being a Thursdaie by the channel by wh wee had entered.

"CHARLES TARLTON."

E S N W

Evil roc[k]

Beacon

Lonely reefs where seabirds fish.

Nun's Point

lonely hut.

The merchant Shipping harbour.

The new Town.

The City of Santa Barbar[a]

. R. H. Sauter / fecit.